Praise for *The Deepening Shade*

"Jake Hinkson is the kind of storyteller who picks the reader up by the ankles and shakes their heart out through their throat. *The Deepening Shade* is the best short story collection I've read in years."

—Benjamin Whitmer, author of
Pike and *Cry Father*

"Collectively, these stories are a feat of black magic conjured by a master wordsmith and story-teller intimate with both the dark side and the resiliency of humanity."

—Eric Rickstad, author of
Reap and *The Silent Girls*

THE DEEPENING SHADE

OTHER TITLES BY JAKE HINKSON

Fiction
Hell on Church Street
The Posthumous Man
Saint Homicide
The Big Ugly
No Tomorrow

Non-Fiction
The Blind Alley: Investigating Film Noir's Forgotten Corners

JAKE HINKSON

THE DEEPENING SHADE

SHADE

NEW AND COLLECTED STORIES

All Due Respect
An imprint of Down & Out Books
3959 Van Dyke Road, Suite 265
Lutz, FL 33558
DownAndOutBooks.com

Cover design by JT Lindroos

ISBN: 1-948235-28-5
ISBN-13: 978-1-948235-28-0

CONTENTS

For
Lindsey J. Muller,
My Other Brother.

When Jesus was nailed to the cross and hung there in torment, he cried out "God, my God! Why hast thou forsaken me?" He cried out as loud as he could. He thought that his heavenly father had abandoned him. He believed everything he'd ever preached was a lie. The moments before he died, Christ was seized by doubt. Surely that must have been his greatest hardship? God's silence.

—Ingmar Bergman's *Winter Light*

In a dark time, the eye begins to see,
I meet my shadow in the deepening shade...
—Theodore Roethke's "In A Dark Time"

MAKER'S AND COKE

I sat up with a start and called out Ellie's name. Our empty house seemed to absorb the sound like a black hole, and I lay back against the pillows with one arm thrown over her side of the bed. Outside my window, the weak morning sun struggled against a damp cloudbank.

I didn't drink that day. I stayed in bed and watched television. The financial markets all around the world were melting down like nuclear reactors. Two twelve year olds in California had raped and killed a sixty-five-year-old woman. The day before, a jihadist in Afghanistan had thrown himself into a schoolroom full of little girls and killed six of them. In between these horrors, a man came on to tell me that I could be free of sexual dysfunction. Another man came on after him and said I could be rich. Later still, a preacher stared into the camera, stared right at me, and said that the root of my anxiety was my sinful nature. I lay there and took it all in. Outside my window, the light didn't change as the day limped by. The winter sky stayed gray, and when the day was over, the dim speck of the sun burned out like a mashed cigarette dying in a tray of ashes. And still I did not have a drink.

That night on my way to work, however, I stopped

by Knight's Liquor Store.

Mr. Knight was a retired Army sergeant who still wore his gray hair short and read Soldier of Fortune. When I walked in, he looked up from his receipts. "Howdy, Officer Lowell."

I dusted some snow off my shoulders and my badge. "Hey, Mr. Knight."

"How goes the crime-fighting?"

"Okay. How goes the booze trade?"

"They say the economy's on the skids, but folks still need to drink, I guess. Might need it more."

I picked up a bottle of Maker's Mark and a two liter of Coke and took it up front. I said, "I guess you're recession proof."

He looked at me over some smudged half-glasses. "I guess your business is pretty recession proof, too."

I nodded and crossed my arms.

He looked at the Glock on my hip. "You ever have to use that thing?"

"No."

"Really?"

"I've had it out, but I've never discharged it in the line of duty."

"I'll be."

I nodded, and he rang up my whiskey and Coke.

After I paid him, he asked, "Headin' home?"

I caught myself before I told the truth. "Yeah," I said. "Gonna sit on the porch."

He smiled and bagged my bottles. "Well, good. Any day you didn't have to fire that gun is a good day, I guess."

"I'd say so. I don't have any desire to take it out in a hurry, I can tell you that." I looked down at the gun.

"'Course, still…"

He pushed my bag toward me. "Still what?"

I shook my head. "Nothing, I was just thinking. It's funny. I'm a crackerjack shot."

He stared at me over his half-glasses and the thick ball of his nose. "That a fact?"

"Marksman."

"Different thing shooting at somebody real."

"I assume so, but I'm not looking to put it to a test unless I have to."

He took off his glasses and rubbed the crinkled bags under his eyes. "Different thing shooting at somebody real," he said again.

I went outside, stashed the bottles in the trunk and drove over to the station to report in. By midnight, I was parked in the side lot of a gas station looking down Colesville Road at the Metro station, and I hadn't touched that booze in the trunk yet. Beside me, in the passenger's seat, was an empty Chick-fil-A bag and a Styrofoam cup full of melting ice. I watched the buses roll in and out of the Metro station, watched the trains from DC coming and going. I tried not to think of Ellie, but I couldn't stop. She was like a virus eating away at my brain. I couldn't think right. I couldn't hold any thought in my head for more than a second unless I was thinking about her. When I did think of her, my brain would just grind to a halt. The terrible thing, of course, was that there was really nothing left to think about. She wasn't coming back, and that was the all of it. She had said there was no one else, no other guy, and I believed her. It wouldn't really matter if there was someone else, anyway. She didn't love me, and that was the main thing. She'd made that clear enough. She didn't

3

love me. Once I thought about it, I realized no one else loved me, either. I sat there and considered it. There was no one left on this earth who loved me. That wasn't self-pity; it was math. My world had gotten smaller and smaller, year by year, and now that Ellie was gone, it was a world of just me.

Fuck it, I thought. Why think about this shit?

I pulled the patrol car behind the gas station dumpster where no one would see me, got out of the car and opened the trunk, dug out the bottles and went back to my seat and made a tall whiskey and coke. I didn't use much whiskey. Didn't want to get drunk. I just wanted to clear the decks a little, clear my brain out so I could think about other things.

I had a drink. It was good. I finished that cup in about one minute, maybe two. I figured I didn't use enough Maker's. I'd barely tasted it. I stiffened up the drink, drank it slower. Took my time with it and watched the last trains pulling into the Metro station down the hill.

I had a third drink, and maybe a forth, making them a little stronger as I went along. I was still okay, and I wasn't really thinking about Ellie anymore. I was thinking about a girl I had met in college. She was in my Spanish class, and she had black hair and blue eyes, I couldn't remember her name.

I had another drink. I lost count as to the number of drinks. I thought about things. I thought about all the things I'd forgotten, like that girl's name, or the sound of my mother's singing. She had sung to me when I was a kid, but I could no longer recall what her voice sounded like. I couldn't remember Ellie's birthday. I couldn't remember the last time I'd cried. I couldn't remember a lot

4

of the people I'd known. The more I thought about it, the more it seemed like I'd lost most of my life. The days had slipped past, and now they were gone.

"This life is a faithless whore," I said, slurring the words a bit.

I shook my head and rubbed my eyes. Needed to stop drinking soon or I wouldn't be able to make it home. Down at the Metro station, the workers closed the big iron gates for the night. Then I saw something in my rearview mirror. A short old man stepped out of the gas station. He had a funny face, and he was wearing a fleece jacket. I shook my head and turned around in my seat. He was about twenty-five yards away from me. His whole head was weird.

It took me a second. His head was Dick Cheney. He looked around. "C'mon," he said to someone.

Another guy in a Dick Cheney mask came out of the gas station. He was taller than the first. He wore a puffy black jacket and carried a hatchet in his right hand.

"Fuck," I said.

When I spun around in my seat, I dropped my cup. Whiskey and coke exploded all over the place. The seat, the steering wheel, the windows.

"Damn it!"

I looked up in the dripping rearview mirror. The two guys hadn't seen me behind the dumpster yet. The shorter guy was looking around. He was nervous. They were waiting on something. I shook my head, rubbed my eyes. I cursed again and pulled out my Glock.

"Now what?" I said to the empty car. "You gonna go up there and arrest them?"

Then what? Call for back up? Stinking of whiskey?

I hit the steering wheel and jumped when I heard a

gunshot. I looked back at the two Dick Cheneys. There were looking at me because I'd just shot a hole in the roof.

"God damn it," I muttered as I stumbled out of the car.

They took off. I stumbled after them in my soggy shoes and soaked pants, but when I got up to the gas station I heard another gun discharge and felt the inside of my chest change. My insides moved. I turned and a third Dick Cheney stood in the doorway of the gas station. He had fired a handgun. I was too drunk to be scared about that. His arm had jerked back. He righted his arm and aimed at me, and I shot him through one of the eye holes in his mask.

He spun to his left, his arm flying up like he was trying to catch something, and he crashed back into the gas station, knocking over a display of chips. Wobbling over to him, I felt an odd movement in my chest, like a tire deflating. I sat down beside him and pulled off the mask. Half his head came off with it. What was still attached was the freckled face of a teenager.

A man kneeled down next to me. He was a brown-skinned man with a short beard. His name tag displayed the name of the gas station and his name: Ataurraheem.

"Are you okay, officer?" he said.

"How do you say your name?" I asked. I had to pull the words up from my chest. He stared at me a second.

He said something.

I shook my head and leaned back on the linoleum to be more comfortable. Leaning over me, he said he would call the police.

I clutched his hand.

"Please," I said. "Don't go."

"Ra-heem," he said. "My friends call me Ra-heem."

"Raheem, don't go. Don't call them yet."

"You're bleeding," he said. "You're bleeding a lot."

"Wait," I said. "Don't call them till it's...See, I'm drunk. She left and I'm drunk and I just killed a kid. Don't call them till it's too late."

He had soft brown eyes, kind eyes. I held his hand. "Please," I said. "Don't call them till I'm gone. I saved you. Don't call them yet."

He nodded. "Okay, I'll stay with you."

"Thank you," I said.

I had to push that last word out and then my voice sucked down into my chest. All of me seemed to draw into my chest. I closed my eyes, but I held onto his hand until I couldn't feel it anymore.

Then I let go.

THE BIG SISTER

I was shaking my tits at the Friday night crowd when I saw my little sister walk through the back door of The Fur Trap. Cinque, the bouncer, asked her for her ID, and then they talked for a second. Janie must have told him she was looking for me because Cin said something, and Janie looked up at the stage where I was straddling a chair in nothing but high heels and sweat. I spun off the chair, scooped up some moist clumps of cash from the stage, and then with one last jiggle for the boys in the front row, I danced off through the tinsel backdrop.

They cut the song I'd been dancing to, and an awkward silence filled the bar before the crowd started muttering. As I hurried to the dressing room, I heard Ralph fumbling over the loudspeaker, "Uh...that was Miss Dixie Delight, ladies and gentlemen. She'll be back...later, later on in the evening. Up next...let's see..."

A new redhead named Nancy rushed past me, stubbing out the cigarette she'd just lit up. She grumbled as she slipped through the tinsel, "You owe me one."

I heard Ralph boom, "Vanessa Domination, ladies and gentlemen!" as the crowd started to clap and cheer.

I thought about running out to the floor to find Janie, but I didn't want to be mobbed by a bunch of drunk assholes on the way. I kicked off my heels and pulled on some jeans. I was digging through my gym bag for a bra when Janie came through the backdoor.

My sister was seventeen years old, and she didn't look a thing like me. She looked like our mother, as short and shapely as a French fry. Somehow I wound up with all the tits and ass in our family. I loved Janie, of course, but we'd never been close because I'd always felt weird that I was so much better looking than her. That sounds like an arrogant way to think about it, but it's the simple truth. Janie looked like a math nerd, which is what she was—or at least what she had always been. She had a plain face with a small nose, small lips and tiny little ears. She never met a frumpy sweatshirt she didn't like. When she came through the backstage door and caught me topless, I felt weird about being naked for the first time in a very long time.

"The fuck are you doing here?" I said, rummaging through my bag. I couldn't find my stuff, so I picked up a dirty sweatshirt someone had left around and slipped it on. Now we looked more like sisters.

"Elizabeth," she said.

"What?" I walked over to the mirror and picked up a towel and wiped off the top layer of my makeup.

When she didn't say anything, I turned around. She was crying.

I walked over to her. "What?" I said, more gently this time. "What's wrong, Janie?" I braced myself for bad news about Mom, maybe Grandma.

"I need your help," she said. "You have to...you have to come with me."

"What's wrong?"

The door popped open and Ralph came in. He was a

young guy, maybe twenty-five, and he'd dropped out of college to start The Fur Trap. He lived and breathed business, and he had all kinds of big plans to expand The Fur Trap into an adult entertainment empire. Recently, he'd been floating the idea of shooting some pay-per-view online videos starring some of us dancers. I knew where he was going with that idea, but I wasn't looking to become a porn star.

"Dixie," he snapped, "what's the deal with leaving the stage early?"

"This is my sister," I said.

Ralph nodded at her, but he didn't see her. Ralph didn't have much use for anyone who wasn't a paying customer. "What's the deal?" he asked me again.

"I have to go."

"What? Where? I got a hundred horny drunks out there."

"And you have enough girls to cover me for an hour," I said. "I gotta go."

"God damn it."

"Janie," I said. "Wait outside." I jerked my head at the door, and my wide-eyed sister slinked toward it.

When she'd closed the door, I told Ralph, "I have to go. It's my father."

"You told me you don't even know your father."

"I don't, but he contacted us because he's dying of testicular cancer. If I want to see him, I have to go now."

It was a horrible lie, but since I didn't know the old man, I didn't mind telling it. Besides, I knew it would work. Ralph's weak spot—and it was a bad one to have if you're managing strippers—was that he basically thought the human body was gross. He hated to hear about periods or yeast infections, much less anything as terrible as a disease. The girls were always telling him they had diarrhea. He'd send you home just to get you out of his face.

"Go," he told me. "Just go."

"This better be good," I told Janie as we climbed into my car. Turning on the heater, I said, "I'm losing money while we're sitting here."

"I'm in trouble," she said. She was shivering.

"What kind of trouble?"

She shook her head.

I stared at her and waited. Our frosty breaths puffed out between us like we were smoking cigarettes.

She said, "I think I killed some...somebody."

"You think you killed somebody."

"Yes."

I leaned closer to her as her breath steamed out through her mouth. She bit her lip.

"Have you been drinking?" I asked.

"Yes."

"What?"

"I don't know. Liquor of some kind."

"Where?"

"At Wendy's apartment."

"Wendy."

Wendy was a twenty-two-year-old high school drop-out who Mom and I didn't like. She was an obnoxious deadbeat pothead, but for some reason my little sister thought she was cool.

I put the car in drive. "Where am I going?" I asked. "Wendy's apartment?"

"Yes."

I pulled out of the parking lot. "Tell me what happened."

"Me and Wendy met this guy at the liquor store—"

"That's fucking great," I said. "You met a guy at the liquor store."

"And we went back to Wendy's apartment."

I felt the skin on my neck and back tighten up.

Janie looked down at her hands. "We were hanging out and drinking, and he started getting loud. He and Wendy started having a fight, but then they made up and went back to her room. I was watching TV. They were in her room having sex."

I hurried through a yellow light and adjusted my rearview mirror to see if there were any cops around.

"I fell asleep on the couch," Janie said, "and then I woke up, and he was there."

"Who is this guy?"

"I don't know. He said his name was Gene."

Wendy's apartment complex was a big place that stretched out over a city block. I'd dropped off Janie there a couple of times, so I knew where I was going, but I pulled into the Walmart parking lot across from the complex and parked at the far end, away from Wendy's apartment.

"Her apartment's down there," Janie told me.

"We'll walk it," I said. "First, you tell me what happened. This asshole woke you up. Then what?"

She looked down at her small, thin hands. I looked at them too, and I don't know why, but just then I remembered teaching her how to snap her fingers when she was little.

"He wanted me to, uh, give him a blow job," Janie said. She was embarrassed to even say the words, and then her face went flush and one by one, tears fell from her eyes.

"You fought him," I said.

She shook her head. "No."

I stared at her.

"Oh."

"Then Wendy came out and found us, and she was really mad and drunk and she started yelling at him. He started yelling at her. I said that maybe I should leave, but they both ignored me. Then he hit her and things got really scary. Wendy lost her mind. She started yelling, and he hit her again, so I ran over and hit him, too."

She stopped and looked out the window. The sky was black and clouded over. There was no moon and no stars.

"What happened then?" I said.

She shook her head. "It just got crazy. He had this gun in his coat, a little gun in his pocket, and when he pulled it out I just...ran. He grabbed me and threw me in the kitchen. Some steak knives fell over." Her tears hit her jeans, and she wiped them away. "And I guess I picked up one and stabbed him."

"You 'guess' or you did?"

She nodded as if to answer. Then she said, "Wendy sent me to get you."

We got out of the car and walked over to Wendy's apartment. It was quiet as we walked down an alley between two rows of townhouses. Wendy's apartment was in a cluster of single-bedroom apartments. Her place was on the bottom, at the end facing the dumpsters, so we came at it from the back alley. We didn't see anyone except a scrawny tomcat digging into a crumpled up Arby's bag.

I tapped on Wendy's door.

14

After a while, a tiny voice said, "Yeah." I looked at the peephole and saw it go dark as Wendy leaned in to look at us.

The door opened, and Wendy hid behind it in the darkened hallway. The only light in the apartment came from the kitchenette. When Janie and I walked in, Wendy shut the door. She was a tubby girl with flabby tits boosted up through the low neckline of her shirt. At twenty-five, she still had acne. Right now, though, except for a swelling black eye, she was as white as a toilet seat.

"Elizabeth," she sighed.

"Where is he?" I asked.

She started crying.

"Christ," I muttered. The apartment wasn't big, so I moved in the direction of the light. Around the edge of the refrigerator, I saw a cowboy boot peeking out. Then I heard a wheeze of breath, and the boot moved.

The two frightened girls behind me both gasped. They huddled against the front door.

I stepped into the kitchenette and found the man lying in a sticky mass of piss and blood. It smelled foul. His face was covered in blood, and I couldn't tell how old he was. One of his eyes was plastered shut with drying blood, but his other eye was open and staring at the kitchen light like it was the face of god.

"Why haven't you called an ambulance?" I asked.

The girls started crying again, and I told them to shut up. I rubbed my face and squatted down beside the dying man, trying not to step in the blood and urine. His small black revolver had skittered into the corner and lay there against the trashcan. Looking down at his face, I didn't feel a goddamn thing. I wasn't terrified, horrified, or anything at all.

15

I tried to think it through as calmly as I could. We could get rid of the body, dump it somewhere, and then hope he didn't get traced back here, but the more I turned that idea over in my head the less sense it made. The cops would trace him back here. It stood to reason. The girls met him at a liquor store. The manger would remember them. They were probably on security cameras.

"You should call the cops," I said.

"No!" Wendy cried. She rushed to the edge of the carpet, not touching the tile in the kitchenette. "They'll... we'll be in trouble."

I stood up. "You got a dying man here," I said. "What do you want to do, bury him in the woods? You think they won't look for him? You think they won't find him? He's not dead yet. If we save him, this won't be as bad. It'll still be bad, but, god, it won't be murder. It was self-defense."

Wendy glanced at the kitchenette counter beside me. She tried to act like she hadn't, but she was too stupid to be subtle. I looked down and saw it. Next to a folded green Army jacket was a man's wallet. I stared at it for a long time.

Then I looked back up at the girls. Behind Wendy, my sister slid down to the carpet as if her legs were useless. She hugged her knees to her chest and stared at the floor. She nodded.

"We tried to steal it," she said.

Wendy swung her head toward Janie, but she didn't say anything. When she looked back at me, I saw all of it there on her stupid face. They'd tried to get this guy drunk and rip him off.

I closed my eyes. I could hear the guy's breathing. I could hear Janie, too, as she rocked back and forth against the front door.

I told Wendy to call 911. "Tell them he attacked you," I said. "Cry. Cry a lot. Then hang up, even if they tell you to stay on the line."

Without another word, Wendy dialed 911 and went to pieces talking to the operator. She even flubbed her own address a couple of times before she got it right. She rubbed her pimply chin, and Janie stared at the floor and rocked back and forth. I watched both of them and waited, knowing that we had to call the cops, but also feeling a sick rumble in my stomach tell me that we couldn't let this guy report his side of the story. When Wendy got done talking to the operator, I told her to wait by the door with Janie.

I walked back into the kitchenette, made sure the girls couldn't see me, and looked down at the man. He wore a flannel shirt and blue jeans, both of which were soaked through with blood. Red bubbles popped out of his left nostril every few seconds. I reached down and pinched his nose. He jerked a bit, but he was so near death he couldn't even lift his arms. In thirty seconds or so, he was dead.

I checked my shoes, arms, legs. The only blood on me was on my thumb and forefinger. I hurried to the bathroom and rinsed them off in the toilet and then flushed the dead man's blood. I washed my hands with a sliver of soap from the shower, and when I was done, I flushed the soap.

I went back out to the girls. They were both standing and staring at me like befuddled old women. I picked up the dead man's wallet, careful to touch it at the edges, and put it in his coat.

"I'm leaving," I said. Janie opened her mouth, but I

raised my hand. "We don't have any time to waste. Shut up and listen. If they know I was here then they'll know you came and got me. That just makes you look bad. That's second-degree murder. At least. You guys have to tell the story. You were hanging out with this older guy. He got rough and brought out a gun. You fought back, and he ended up stabbed. You were in shock. You didn't know what to do. Finally, you called 911. He died before they got here. That's it. I wasn't here. And you didn't leave."

Wendy said, "What if—"

"There's a thousand what if's," I told her. "Stick to that story no matter what. Be as nonspecific on the time as you can be, but don't specifically lie."

Janie nodded.

Wendy said, "Okay."

I stepped to the door, and Janie reached out and took my arm. I looked at her and patted her hand. "Just stick to the story," I said.

I slipped out, crept back down the alley and went to my car. I was back at The Fur Trap in a few minutes.

"How's your dad?" Ralph sneered when I walked backstage.

"He's okay," I said taking off my sweatshirt.

"You're full of shit, you know."

"I know."

"Who was that girl, really?"

"My coke connection," I said, shimmying out of my jeans.

"Get out of here. It was not."

I shrugged and walked over to the mirror to put on some makeup. He walked up behind me. I stopped what I was doing and looked at him over my shoulder in the mirror. He was staring at me, thinking hard about something. I hated that sleazy little motherfucker.

"Where'd you go?" he asked.

"Nowhere," I said. "I've been here all night. Out in the parking lot doing blow."

"Yeah?"

"Yeah."

He stared at me, his little blue eyes like pieces of ice. Maybe I didn't come across as nonchalant as I thought. "Okay, Dixie Delight," he said, "but you owe me."

"What do I owe you?"

"I don't know yet. Depends on where you really were for the last hour. You might owe me a lot."

"I told you where I was."

He nodded. "Sure. Let's just call it a rain check, okay?"

"What do you want, Ralph? Private dance? Sloppy blowjob back in your office? You ain't getting either one, you know."

He smiled an ugly smile. "You ain't my type, Dixie. I like decent girls. I'll tell you what though, when I start that online sideline next month...you might think about what you owe me."

He patted my shoulder and walked away. For a while, I sat there in the empty backroom, staring at the door. Then I looked at myself in the mirror. I don't know what I saw. Not a murderer. Not a stripper. Not even an older sister. I just saw a worried woman. I stared at her for a second, and then I caked some makeup on her face.

THE GIRL FROM YESTERDAY

She was pregnant but terribly underweight at the same time, with a black eye starting to go purple and hunger chapping her bruised lips. The guy with her didn't look like the type of guy to knock around a pregnant girl, but you can never tell. He was balding and quiet, wearing dirty black slacks with holes in the knees. I was willing to bet they were both dressed entirely in clothing they'd picked up at shelters like ours. The guy looked fifty or even sixty. The girl was about nineteen.

I was hanging up my office phone as they sat down at one of the long tables. I'd been watching them since they walked in the door. It was noon and the shelter was full of drunks trying to hold off their drinking until after lunch. My partner, Betty, was in the kitchen and I could see her through what had once been the order window when our mission was still a restaurant. Her graying hair was pulled back in a no-nonsense ponytail —just like mine—and she was barking orders at someone behind her in the kitchen. When she yells, Betty still looks like the twenty-year-old girl I fell in love with.

I got up and walked to the door of my office. The pregnant girl and her man sat down at one of the tables by the exit. The volunteers from the African Methodist

Episcopal Church, most of them teenagers, were passing out the bowls of stew. A kid named Nate—a nice kid with a big funky afro—was cutting up pans of cornbread into little squares. He was cutting them up too small, probably because Betty had told him the day before that he was cutting them too big. He loaded the slices onto a tray and started passing them out. The pregnant girl ate her little square of cornbread as soon as Nate handed it to her.

I was smoking a cigarette. Betty didn't like me to smoke and especially didn't like me to smoke in the shelter, but I…well, I don't have a good way to finish that sentence. I guess I'm ornery sometimes, but if you're in the sad business of trying to reduce human suffering, much of it self-inflicted, you've seen enough hunger and sorrow—and you've taken enough punches in the jaw by quivering junkies who don't care if you're old enough to be their mother—to get a little ornery sometimes.

I mashed out my cigarette and dropped it in a Coke can. The pregnant girl was tearing into her stew, but the old guy with her just stared at the tablecloth.

I walked over to their table.

The girl didn't stop eating, and the old guy didn't stop staring at the tablecloth. He wasn't drunk though. I can spot a drunk from many miles away. His problem was that he wasn't right in the head. I see a lot of guys who aren't right in the head, too.

Lonnie, a regular who's drunk twenty-three out of every twenty-four hours, was sitting next to the girl. He was wearing red sweatpants and a brand new t-shirt with an American flag on the front.

"Howdy, Marie," he said.

"Lonnie," I said. "How goes it?"

"Pretty well. Stew's hot."

"Betty keeps the pots burning," I said.

"She don't like me," Lonnie said.

I shrugged. Betty probably didn't like Lonnie. "She got up this morning and spent the day making you stew, didn't she?" I asked. "What were you doing at nine o'clock this morning?"

Lonnie smiled a gappy grin. "Sleeping down by the river."

"Drunk?"

Lonnie shrugged. "Beats thinking."

The girl and her man had not changed what they were doing this whole time. She finished her stew and reached for his. He didn't flinch as she took it. She patted his shoulder and started into the stew.

I sat down.

"Hello," I said to her. I could tell he wasn't much of a talker.

She nodded and kept eating, getting faster at it like she thought I might take it away.

"Marie Porter," I said. "I run this place with my partner Betty."

The girl nodded.

"What's your name?" I asked. No harm in asking.

"Rita," she lied. She took a long pull off of her glass of water.

I nodded. "Haven't seen you here before."

"Passing through," she said.

"Who's your friend, Rita?"

She put down her spoon. "Why are you asking me these questions?"

I shrugged.

She looked at the old man. He was a dirty character.

Grime filled the grooves of his rough face. Now that I was closer to him, I was pretty sure he was actually younger than I'd first thought.

Without taking his gaze from the tablecloth, he touched his forehead, and I noticed for the first time some bruises at his receded hairline.

"What happened?" I asked him.

He shook his head. One of his eyeballs was bloody.

The girl looked around as if she was starting to get scared.

"Why don't we go sit in my office?" I said.

The girl wasn't happy about it and looked at the old man for a sign of what to do. He touched his forehead again and tears welled up in the girl's blue eyes.

I led them to the office. The old guy shuffled, but the girl had a bizarrely quick step, as if she'd been walking so long she'd forgotten she was pregnant.

I motioned at the two chairs in front of my desk and walked around it, sat down and closed the spread out newspaper. I dropped it beside my swivel chair.

"What happened, Rita?"

"We were attacked a couple of days ago."

"Attacked where?"

She shrugged. "I don't know. Downtown. We were coming up here from Texas and our car broke down."

"Where were you going?"

"North."

"I assumed you were heading north if you came up from Texas," I said, "but where up north?"

She looked at the old man as if she expected him to answer. She tapped her stubby, dirty fingernails on the seat, and he didn't move. "He hasn't been right for a couple days," she said.

"So what happened a couple of days ago?"

"Our car broke down. He couldn't fix it because he didn't have the right part. The Lord led us down to the river."

I nodded. Between the two of us, Betty is the religious one. Before we got together she made something exceedingly clear. "I'm going to serve god until the day I die," she said. Betty believes in god. I believe in Betty.

I asked Rita, "What happened at the river?"

"We slept there a couple of days."

I nodded at the old man. "What's his name?"

She looked at him. He was staring at my desk like it was whispering something to him he couldn't quite hear.

Rita said, "He is the one the Lord calls The Revelator." When she said it, she sounded like an automated phone operator.

"I see," I said. "So you and the, uh, Revelator here were down at the river and then what?"

"A man came," she said.

"Who was this man?"

She shook her head. "I'm not sure. The Revelator was suspicious of him from the beginning."

"Was he a homeless man?"

"No."

"How do you know?"

"We had seen him a few days before," she said, letting out a sigh that was all exhaustion and no attitude. Then, "We were getting food out of a dumpster behind a restaurant, a Mexican food place. This man came out of the back door and told us to go away. The Revelator told him that as God had fed Elijah in the wilderness, causing the ravens to bring him meat and bread, that" she tumbled over the words "that he, that God would provide for the Revelator and his bride. The ravens would come for us."

"You're married?" I said.

She nodded.

"You don't have a ring," I said.

"We were married by God, not by Man," she said.

"Oh. And then what happened?"

"We left and went back to the river. The next day, or maybe two days, I don't know, the man came down to the river."

"Why?"

She shook her head. "He wanted to take me away from the Revelator."

"He wanted to take you where?"

She shook her head and looked at the Revelator. The Revelator was asleep.

"Where did he want to take you?" I asked.

"To hell. He wanted to stop the Revelator from finishing his work. The Lord hath decreed that the Revelator should take his bride and hasten the second coming."

I nodded. "And what would happen if you were taken away?"

She sat up very straight in the chair. She paid so little mind to her swollen stomach it was as if she wasn't aware of it. "The Revelator and his bride are one body. No one shall separate the body without destroying it. The Lord hath decreed the bride of the Revelator should burn in the lake of fire with the Deceiver if she be taken away from him. The bride's family should die the deaths of the heathen and darkness should fall on the face of the earth."

I looked at the Revelator. A line of spit was running down his chin. There looked to be a little blood in it.

26

She said, "The evil man wanted to take me away, to men with guns. The Revelator struggled with him, but the Deceiver was strong with the man and he" her voice cracked "he hit the Revelator with a pipe."

"What did you do, Rita?"

She shook her head.

"Please tell me," I said. "What did you do? The man hit the Revelator with this pipe, hit him on the head it looks like."

"Yes," she said, wiping her tears. "Several times. Hit him." She shook her head and put her knuckle to her mouth. "I didn't know what to do. My mother…"

"You were afraid the man with the pipe was going to take you away from the Revelator."

"Yes. And the Lord hath decreed that the bride's family should die the deaths of heathens if she be taken away." She sighed again. "Or run away."

"So you protected the Revelator?"

"Yes. We had a knife in our bag. It was long and thin. I drew it across the evil man's neck as the Revelator had taught me."

"You'd done this before?"

"No," she shook her head. "But the Revelator showed me how."

"I see. Then what?"

"I put the man in the river. But" she choked up again and touched the Revelator lightly, almost maternally, on the arm "but he wasn't…right. He'd always said we should avoid the heathen and their places but, but I was so hungry. I was so hungry, and the ravens never came to us."

I nodded. I picked up the paper and opened it and slid it across the table.

It was yesterday's paper. Under a picture of Rita, taken some years earlier when she was clean and young and smiling at the camera like she was thinking of what she was going to wear to prom, a headline read, "Karen Nelson, Missing for Three Years from Church Youth Trip, Seen in Texarkana Two Days Ago. Police: 'This is the Best Lead in Years.'" Next to the text of the article was a picture of Rita and the Revelator standing at the counter of a gas station in Texarkana.

Rita looked at it. Behind her I saw four uniformed officers walk in. I was impressed with how quickly they'd responded to my phone call. One walked over to the kitchen window. The drunks and homeless souls sitting at the tables all stiffened up. Betty, her eyes wide with alarm, pointed the cop to my office. Her hazel eyes met mine, and I tried to smile reassuringly.

"There are people here," I said. "They want to talk to you, Rita. They're going to take you and the Revelator to the hospital. He needs his head looked at where the man hit him with that pipe. And you need your baby looked at."

She regarded her stomach for the first time. "I don't want them to take my baby away from me."

"They won't," I said. I stood up. The cops were at the door. One, a handsome, silver-haired guy, came in slowly.

Rita turned and when she saw them she screamed. The cops poured into the room and tackled the Revelator. They threw him to the ground, and he kicked a little. He wasn't really even awake, but they held him down despite his lack of struggle. One of the cops was a stocky blonde with a hard mouth. While the guys subdued the unconscious man on the floor, she put some handcuffs on Rita before I could see her do it.

28

"She doesn't need those," I barked.

"Back up, ma'am," the cop barked back.

The cop with the silver hair jumped up and clapped his thick hand on my shoulder. "You need to calm down, ma'am," he said.

Betty was in the doorway. Her hair was pulled back in a scarf, and sweat beaded her face.

I took a deep breath. Rita had crumbled to the floor. I said, "I am calm sir. I think the girl is already very agitated, and she doesn't require handcuffs."

The cops were pulling the Revelator to his feet. Rita was turning red. "Don't hurt him," she said.

I knelt down next to her and put my arms around her. She sunk into me. "He'll be okay, Rita," I said.

The silver-haired cop knelt down. His voice was soft, and he seemed to be following my lead now. "Ma'am," he said.

"Don't hurt him," she said.

"We won't hurt him," the cop said. The others had pulled the Revelator up and put him back in the chair. "I need to ask you some questions."

The girl wouldn't look at him. Her face was buried in my chest.

"Are you Karen Ann Nelson?"

She shook her head.

"Tell him the truth, Rita," I said.

The cop said, "Are you Karen Ann Nelson of Arlington, Texas?"

Rita drew her head up and looked at me. "That was the name Man gave me," she said. "God hath given me another name in heaven."

"Good Lord," Betty said.

The cop frowned and looked at me. Then he pointed

29

at the Revelator and asked Rita, "Who is this man?"

She stared at the drooling old man and touched her stomach. "The flesh of my flesh," she said.

RANDY'S PERSONAL LORD AND SAVIOR

I can't remember anyone proselytizing to me before I moved down to Arkansas. I knew Catholics who dabbed ashes on their foreheads once a year, and Jews who wore yarmulkes, and Muslims who fasted during Ramadan, but I never met anyone who really took it upon themselves to show me the light until I moved from Chicago to Little Rock. That's where I met Randy.

We met as galley slaves down in the customer service bowels at Alltel. Our cubicles sat across from one another. Geek shit decorated mine: a couple of plastic doodads from Happy Meals, a Princess Leia Queen of Hearts from a long lost deck of Star Wars playing cards, a small Batman poster.

Randy's cubicle contrasted mine in nearly every way. Whereas scattered forms covered my desk like pieces of a puzzle I needed to finish, his papers were stacked, his computer screen never had a dust mote on it, and his walls were bare except for two things. He had the exact same Batman poster as me, and he had a bumper sticker stuck in the top corner of his wall, where everyone who passed could read: Ask Me About Jesus.

My first day at work we shook hands and said hello and didn't have time for much else. I was still learning the ropes, so I kept my head down and concentrated on the job. Randy didn't have much time either because he was Mister Employee of the Month. Sitting ramrod straight at his computer, headset clamped tight on his blond buzz cut, he performed customer service like it was his life's highest ambition. At lunch he shot me with thumb and forefinger as I was heading to the break room, and when I got back an hour later he was still at his computer, straight as a statue saying, "Well, thank you, ma'am. We always appreciate the call."

A week or so after I started there he leaned against my cubicle one day and said, "Batman poster, huh?"

"You bet."

"Got the same thing, dude." He jerked his thumb over his shoulder.

"Yeah, I saw. Pretty cool."

He nodded.

I nodded back.

Randy straightened up and rotated his thick shoulders. "Back's all tensed up. This work's tough on the ole trapezius. I used to be in the Army, and they worked us hard, but this sitting at a desk is its own kind of complaint."

I nodded.

He said, "You find that to be true, man?"

"I slouch," I said. "Compensates. Evens things out a little."

Randy smiled. "Yeah. Okay, buddy, I got to jump back on the phones. Let me know if there's any way I can help you adjust."

I said I would, and we went back to work.

Three days later I was passing him a box of staples when, for the hell of it, I jerked my head at his Jesus sticker and said, "So Randy, what can you tell me about this Mexican?"

"Sanchez in accounting? I think she's Catholic."

"No," I said. I pointed at his sticker. "This Jesus guy."

He stared at me for a second before he smiled. Then he shook his head. "Be happy to share with you all I know, man."

"Hit me."

I don't know why I brought it up. For as long as I can remember I've always suspected that religion is just the illusion of certainty, a security blanket in an insecure world. But there's nothing more dangerous than relieving people of their illusions, and, besides, I wasn't nearly presumptuous enough to want to set Randy straight on his worldview, anyway. I suppose I just wanted to hear his pitch. I mean, he had the sticker. He obviously wanted to give people the pitch.

He spread his palms out. "Jesus is my personal lord and savior."

"As opposed to impersonal?"

"Yep," he said. "Totally personal."

"Custom made?"

Randy smiled and shot me with his forefinger. He knew I was riding him a little, but he was too good a salesman not to use that for an in. "All custom, dude. Like your relationship with that special lady in your life. It's a beautiful thing, right?"

"Sure," I said. I'd been bereft of a special lady for a while, but why burden Randy with that?

"Same with Jesus, man. He's looking for that totally personal, totally unique relationship with you. You and only you."

I nodded. We were quickly getting to a point in the conversation where I was going to run out of anything to say that wasn't more sarcastic than the last thing I'd said.

"Well, that's cool."

"Listen," Randy said, "this isn't a small thing. I'm telling you right now that Jesus turned my life around. I was out there stumbling in the dark like a fool and he picked me up and turned on the lights. Jesus made it happen for me."

"Yeah," I said. I turned a little in my chair and lifted my hand to gesture at my desk. Well got to get back to...

He didn't notice. He was too locked in, and now I was getting nervous. I could feel myself becoming embarrassed, though I would have been hard pressed to explain why.

"There's stuff to tell, dude," Randy said. "I was wicked. I was a bad guy, really and truly, out there doing things I'm not at all proud of."

I could see Randy wearing a bra on his head at a kegger with his slobbery frat brothers, stocking up on all the guilt he'd need to become born again someday. I smiled and nodded. Mister Understanding.

He just rubbed his hands together. "I'll tell you all about it someday, dude. You'll see. Jesus done turned my thing all around."

After that we didn't talk about the whole Jesus business for a while. Randy was, as always, at the computer, taking calls and firing off emails and faxes. I suppose I was doing the same thing, but at a more casual pace.

Then in early December we found ourselves being surly on the same couch at the company Christmas party. I was surly because I was at a company Christmas party, which was more or less mandatory. Randy was surly because everyone was drinking.

There were a few hundred people there, nobody too important or too high up the food chain, and we were all crammed into the main lobby of the building. There were long tables set up with cold cuts and punch, a couple of desserts, and a stock of mediocre wine.

I wasn't drinking because I don't really like wine. Randy leaned over and asked, "You don't drink?"

I shrugged. "Beer's about all I can handle."

He nodded.

"You?" I asked.

"Naw, man. Jesus weaned me off the grape. Drinking a bunch of alcohol ain't what the Lord intended."

I said, "Come on, Randy, how do you know what God intends?"

"Holy Spirit, dude."

"The Holy Spirit?"

"Totally. Bible says the Holy Spirit makes all things known."

"All things being known, shouldn't you be shift supervisor or something?"

He leaned back into the cushions, crossing his legs. His tie was loose, his thick, tan neck exposed. "I don't claim to know everything. If that came off as arrogant it's not how I meant it. I just meant that the Lord makes his mysteries known to us, a lot of them anyway. The things I don't know are things I don't know because I'm not righteous enough yet to grasp them. That's all I'm saying."

"We could be getting drunk right now," I pointed out. I was rethinking my no-wine policy.

"Go ahead, dude. I ain't touching it. Can't believe they'd serve it at a company function. At a Christmas party even."

I scooted to the edge of the sofa. "Last chance," I said. "Just one?"

"You ever see that movie The Passion of the Christ?" he asked.

"No," I said. "That's the real violent one, right?"

"Yeah," he said, "and Jesus didn't take that kind of butt whooping so I could sit here getting sloshed at his birthday party."

I got up and grabbed a plastic cup of some cheap red. When I got back over to Randy he was looking at the bottom of his shoes.

"Have you ever taken a drink?" I asked, sitting down.

He picked at the shoe with his fingernail and nodded. "Time or two."

"How'd that work out for you?"

"Not too well."

I looked at him. He looked at the bottom of his shoe. I said, "You seem depressed all the sudden."

He shook his head. "Naw. I've fought depression before. Had it bad for a while. This is just me being bummed out that the world ain't what it should be."

"When were you depressed?"

"Couple years ago, about the time I come back from overseas."

"Where were you stationed?"

"Germany."

"How was that?"

He shrugged. "It was okay. I'm not much for foreign

places. I like America, you know?"

I took a sip of wine. It wasn't mediocre; it was bad. I drank some more.

Randy said, "Had a crap job over in Germany, man."

"Which was?"

"Which was me and this other dude had to escort the coffins off the planes when the bodies came in from Iraq."

"Really?"

"Yeah. It was like a little funeral every time. Depressing, dude. Gets you down."

"I bet."

He nodded.

"So that was why you got depressed?" I asked.

He shrugged. "I guess. I tried to deal with it in unproductive ways. Me and this other dude, Daniels, we would go out drinking after work, and, I mean, those Germans like the booze, man. Me and Daniels would just be drunk twenty-four/seven when we weren't working. It's all we did. Kind of. I mean a lot of times we'd be out looking for young ladies. Only we didn't call them that, young ladies, and we didn't think of them that way. We only thought of them as girls we were trying to pick up. And we did. We did pick them up."

"German girls?"

"Not usually. Usually they were military chicks—young ladies, and we'd just use them."

"So you were getting drunk and getting laid. Sounds like nearly every military guy I've ever known, Randy."

He rubbed his face. "That's no kind of excuse though, man."

I finished my wine. I stood up to get some more but first I told him, "Most women know the score, Randy. You can't be used by someone unless you let them use you. And, also, it goes both ways. Those girls were using you, too. Think about that."

I left him thinking and went and loaded up on some more wine. I hit the snack table, got a plate of carrots and celery, and headed back to Randy.

I offered him a carrot and he waved it away. "No thanks. But here's the thing, man, we did use those girls."

I ate some celery. "I'm not saying you weren't being a douchebag, Randy. I'm sure you were being a colossal douchebag, but women are equal to men—up to and including their ability to decide who they drunkenly fuck in the backseat of a jeep. Or wherever."

He looked at the bottom of his shoe again and picked at it like a scab. I sipped some wine. He said, "What if they didn't decide?"

"What do you mean?"

He shook his head. "Nothing," he muttered.

"What do you mean? How could they not decide?"

He took a deep breath. "There was this young lady in artillery named McKenty. She was this big-hipped red-head from Durham, North Carolina. Real cute. Had a thing for ugly guys, though. Dated every ugly joe on the base. Uglier the better it seemed like.

"So one night me and Daniels run into her at the bar. She's there drinking alone, which was kind of odd because McKenty usually had somebody with her. The guys were all over her all the time." Randy clicked his teeth together. "That must have been annoying." He shrugged. "Anyway, she usually had some dude hitting on her cause she was pretty much a sure thing. You know what I'm saying?"

"I guess," I said.

"But she was alone that night, so me and Daniels just

plopped down and started buying her drinks. We were drinking, too, of course, but McKenty was pouring it down like a sink. She held it pretty good, too, but she was kinda bummed out the whole time. Which wasn't like her, you know? She was always a good time. It wasn't just that she was easy, although I guess that's what we mostly cared about, but she was pretty cool, too."

"Cool how?"

He frowned and shook his head. "I mean, she could be pretty funny. And she was always talking up Raleigh-Durham like it was this great place and telling you cool stories about her grandpa who used to be some kind of Appalachian moonshiner. Stuff like that. And she was good at darts."

"Okay," I said.

He watched Vanessa Sanchez loading up her plate with kiwi and strawberries. I didn't want to say anything, but I didn't want his mind to wander too far, either.

"Okay," I said again. "So what happened that night with McKenty at the bar?"

He waved it away. "The past. I shouldn't trudge it up."

If I were nice I would have let it go there, but I guess I'm not nice. I wanted him to finish. I pulled out my ace card. "I thought you were giving me the rundown on Jesus," I said.

"Yeah," he said.

"Or is Christianity just all cookouts and bumper stickers?"

It was an asshole thing to say, but Randy looked like I'd thrown cold water on him. "No, man. Jesus is the real deal. I mean, there ain't nothing more real."

"Then come across with the story, man. What

happened with McKenty?"

He sighed. "We got her drunk. You figured that already. She was real sad and just wanted to drink, I guess, so we kept pouring the drinks down her. That lasted till about closing time. She was slobbering then, just barely awake, and we took her for a drive. We went down to this sort of junkyard place by a stream at the far end of the airfield. It was gross down there. The water was all yellow and dirty from the rusted metal and stuff."

I nodded. A guy from accounting started playing around on a piano by the stairs.

Over the opening bars of "O Holy Night," Randy said, "We had one of those green army blankets. It was heavy duty, real scratchy and uncomfortable. We laid it down by some old tires."

He shrugged.

I waited.

"You know," he said.

I shook my head.

He nodded. "Come on, you know."

"No," I said, "I don't."

"We had sex with her."

I sipped my wine.

He stared down at the floor. "I can't believe I'm telling you this. She wasn't even really sure what was going on. After we got done she was kinda halfway awake and she started throwing up in that nasty water."

I sat back on the sofa. Randy looked at me. "Pretty awful," he said. "Pretty bad. We took her back to her apartment. She lived off base with this other girl. We dropped her off."

"Did you see her after that?"

"Sure. Every day. She never said anything about it."

I shook my head.

"Yeah," Randy said. "I felt bad about it. I did. Messed me up for a while there until I met Jesus. I needed him to help me with the guilt."

Something seemed off about him. He'd sounded like he felt guilty up to the moment he'd said he felt guilty, but then he sounded like he was reading it from a sheet of paper.

I had a hunch. "Guilty for what?" I asked.

"For what we done, what I told you about."

"But which part exactly?"

He rubbed his thick neck and sighed. "All of it. Drinking, sex." He shook his head. "Two guys...We didn't touch each other, don't get me wrong. But two men seeing each other like that, that ain't right."

"I see," I said. "What about her being drunk?"

Randy held out his hands. "Yeah, I don't feel good about that, but McKenty was kinda the type for that, you know."

"The type to be raped?"

He shook his head. "Whoa. No, dude. No. We didn't...we didn't do that."

"It sort of sounded that way."

He shook his head and his big hands closed into fists. He leaned close to me, and I could see a small scar cutting across his left eyebrow. "No no no. You heard it wrong or something. She wasn't fighting nobody off. She wasn't saying no. And she wasn't the kind to say no, you know what I mean? If she had been sober she would have been the kind of girl to rock and roll on a deal like that."

"Like you."

Randy leaned back and took a deep breath. "Thing

41

is, I was under the influence of the devil."

"C'mon, man..."

"You don't believe in the devil?"

"No."

He looked at me like I was a cancer patient smoking a cigarette. "Jesus believed in the devil," he said. "Believed in him, talked to him, fought him."

"You really believe that?"

"Sure as you're sitting there."

"You're as sure of the existence of the devil as you are of the fact that I'm sitting here."

"More."

"More?" I said. The word dropped out of my mouth like a turd.

"Yep. Cause the Bible says it."

"It says a lot of things, Randy."

He shook his head and waved my words away. Again he moved close to me. "Look, I'm cool having this discussion with you. I don't mind telling you my story. I told you I was a sinner, but I'm redeemed. I fell a long ways, but Jesus pulled me up even higher. He had to reach far down into the pit of sin to pull me out, but he did. He did. He pulled me up and lifted me high."

"You sound like a preacher."

Randy shrugged and leaned back and wedged his hands into his pants pockets. "Calling it like I see it. No sugarcoat."

One of the techies, a blonde named Kerri, stumbled over to us a little buzzed and sat down on the coffee table. She slipped off her wobbly heels and put her bare feet on top of my shoes.

"I can read palms," she said, reaching for my hand.

I let her look at it, but Randy was already standing up.

"Good love line," Kerri said. "You're going to marry soon."

"I doubt that," I said.

Randy paused at the elbow of our supervisor, thanked him for the party and headed out the door.

Kerri tickled my palm.

I turned back to her and smiled.

She said, "What happened to the R Man?"

"Went home."

"He's nice," she said. "I like him."

"He loves Jesus," I said.

"Hey, don't we all?"

"No," I said.

Kerri blinked a few times, let go of my hand and poked a long pink fingernail into my kneecap. "Well, he loves you, buddy boy. He loves all of us."

"Do you really believe that?" I asked.

She smiled, but it only made her look kind of sad.

"It'd sure be nice," she said.

AFTERMATH

When the robbers burst in at twelve past twelve on this bright August afternoon, Marianne doesn't notice. Leaning over the tabletop, ignoring her lobster sandwich, she is explaining commodities futures to a potential client. Focused on making her argument, zeroed in on her goal, Marianne does not see that people around her are raising their hands. Conversations lurch and sputter. People begin pulling out their cell phones and holding them in the air. Only when the client breaks eye contact and gasps does Marianne turn to see three men with guns stomping among the fine linen and issuing orders.

Marianne has never been in such physical danger before, but she knows in that instant she is a coward. She pulls out her cell phone from her suit's breast pocket and holds it aloft and looks at the most distant corner of the room. Her concentration flees as far away as possible.

"Don't worry folks," one robber says. "Everyone stay calm and this will be over in a couple of minutes. One of us is going to take the cell phones and one of us is going to collect the wallets. You'll get your cell phones back at the end of this. Everyone stay calm."

The man coming around to collect the cell phones in a black trash bag is composed, even polite. He wears a plastic mask of some kind, though Marianne can't bring herself to look directly at it when the man gets to her. Instead she stares at a drop of condensation on her water glass as a voice, raspy and deep and measured, requests "Cell phone, please, ma'am." When Marianne hands it over, the man snaps it out of her hand and drops it in the bag. Then he moves on.

Another man comes around to collect wallets into another plastic bag. He wears a similar mask, but it seems too tight. He breathes heavily through the slits in the mask and doesn't say anything as he takes Marianne's wallet.

Like a child squeezing her eyes shut to avoid the dark, Marianne continues to focus at the condensation as it drips onto the linen and soaks into the cloth.

Then the oddest thing happens. It happens so slowly, Marianne is forced to see it.

A few feet away from her, an older woman in a business suit, with short gray hair and large red earrings, sticks out her foot and trips the polite robber with the cell phone bag. Then she yells, "C'mon Bill"—speaking perhaps to the terrified little man trembling beside her— and tries to jump on the robber.

It's such an absurd attempt at heroism it angers Marianne. The robber knocks the older woman to the floor, and everyone in the restaurant seems at once to gasp. No one moves to help the woman. No one moves at all. Even the other robbers stop. The polite robber stands up and takes a step toward the woman. She is on her hands and knees, struggling to get to her feet. The robber points his gun at the back of her head and pulls the trigger.

* * *

Everyone has jumped and people are screaming and the woman lies dead on the floor. Marianne, realizing she has a drop of blood in her eye, wipes it away.

The police question everyone. The robbers have fled in a blue Windstar with New Jersey license plates. They dropped the bag of cell phones at the edge of the parking lot, one investigator explains, to avoid the GPS.

Marianne leaves after she is questioned, but she doesn't go back to work. She doesn't say a word to her lunch companion. She doesn't have a wallet or any money. She walks to her car, but the thought of sitting down makes her stomach lurch.

She keeps walking. The riverfront is nearby, so she wanders over to it. The water is idle.

What was that woman thinking? C'mon, Bill.

Who was she? What had led her to that moment? A lifetime of idiocy, perhaps. Maybe she was the stupid person at work who'd always thought too highly of herself.

Or maybe it was the other way around. Maybe she was an amazing human being, one who'd overcome a lifetime of troubles, who'd always come out on top because of pluck and daring.

Either way she is dead now.

Along the Navesink Riverfront people idle, shift, run. Mothers and fathers watch children playing on a swing set. Leaning against the long black railing, two teenagers are locked in an undulating kiss. One old man sits alone on a bench, rubbing his moist eyes.

Marianne walks up to the railing and stares down at the placid surface of the water.

C'mon, Bill.

She climbs over the railing, walks through the weed-pocked mud to the water's edge. Her shoes sink, her slacks absorb the muck. She wades into the water. The mothers and fathers point at her. The couple stops kissing. She wades further in. The mud sucks away one shoe. She wades out until the water, still and calm, rises to her waist. She stares down at the clouds swaying in the river. She slaps the water gently and watches the sky ripple.

THE EMPTY SKY

It's a darn curious thing to go your whole life without children, only to find yourself stuck in a nursing home across the street from a daycare. I sit outside most days with the other old folks, and we watch the children play. Most of the time, it don't bother me.

But I couldn't sleep last night on account of my shoulder hurting. It's the shoulder that's pained me off and on since I fell off our porch the winter I was pregnant. I never had my baby because of that, and even though that was sixty years ago, and I never got to see him, I can still remember how he felt growing inside of me. I been thinking about that today, so I stayed inside.

Some folks say I been alone since I lost my baby, but it's a fact that Jesus has been faithful to stay with me. I ain't saying that I ain't strayed from him, because I have. I've strayed terrible at times. But it's a testament to the sweetness of Him who saved me that He's never left me.

Course now, we always have had evil. It ain't just me. I never knew my Momma or my Daddy because they left me with Margie when I was five, and Margie always told me that they had to split up over Daddy's drinking and wickedness. Margie said Momma never did want any child anyway but at least felt strong enough

49

for me to leave me with a good Christian family.

I lived with Margie and her husband and their three boys in a little sharecropper's one-room in the middle of a hundred acres of strawberries. There was only one bunk in the place—one for Margie and her husband. Me and the boys slept on thick quilts on the floor. We had a little table with two chairs and a gray wood-burning stove with black splotches around the door. I was only about five when I come out there, but I remember on my first day, I sat out in the dirt, between the long rows, and ate Margie's strawberries, red and green and all sour-sweet, till I was sick.

Her husband didn't go with us, but Margie took us kids to the Higher Living Baptist Church ever Sunday. Although she was never too sweet with me, she wasn't too mean neither, and she brought me up right. She never paid me no special attention because, after all, I wasn't one of her own and because she said she never wanted a girl no ways. The day I met her, she already had some gray in her hair, but thirty years later, on the day she died, she still had a few black hairs in there, too. Her face was always strong as a Indian's, and she hoarded her smiles like they cost her money. I never felt too sweet about her when I was a child, but I always respected her.

When I was twenty-one, and still living with Margie, I met Ezra. He was only sixteen, but he was a man of God if ever there was one. He had this thick black hair and clear blue eyes and a voice that was as clean and pure as any singer I ever heard. Some nights, our preacher would ask him to say a few words, and Ezra would start preaching, and you'd swear the apostle Paul himself was standing there.

One day, walking home from church, I told Margie, "Boy, that Ezra can preach, can't he?"

"He's got the Spirit of the Lord," she said nodding. "He's partial to you, too, Clara."

"Oh, he wouldn't look at me," I said. "I ain't nothing to look at." Even while I was saying it, though, I could feel my skin start to goose pimple under my sweat.

"He's mighty young," she said, "but he'd make a good husband."

"He sure would," I said, and something about the way I said it made her laugh.

It was the very next Sunday that he come up to me after service. He was already tall. He smiled down at me and his kind blue eyes was sparkling like a creek in winter-time. I don't suppose anybody short of Jesus ever had eyes that was softer and prettier than Ezra's.

"Can I walk you home, Clara?" he asked, fiddling with the spine of his Bible. "I unnerstand if you need to go with Margie and them."

"No," I told him, "I'll go tell her you're walking me home. She won't mind on account it's you."

We was cutting across a field to get to my road when Ezra stopped and looked down at the grass. It was a little high, up to our ankles, and I was so dumb I thought at first he'd seen a snake or something.

"Ezra…"

"Clara, can I tell you something?"

"Ezra, you all right?"

He looked up at me and took his coat off and there was sweat rings under his arms and he smiled all shy at me. I walked over to him and put my hand on his thick arm.

"I know you think I'm just a boy," he said.

"I don't think that," I told him. "I think you're a man, a good man of God."

"Do you think I could come to see you tomorrow?"

"Yes," I said taking his hand.

The next week or so was the happiest days of my life. We was so fond of each other and ever body talked about us. Ezra came up to the house to see me ever other day, and he and I would stroll through the strawberries and hold hands and talk about the future.

He'd say he loved me.

Oh! and the shock that would give me ever time! Ever time was just like the first. I'd stare down at the wiry green vines at our feet and tell him, "I love you, too, Ezra."

"I'm gonna be a preacher," he'd say.

"You'll be a fine one," I'd say.

"Preacher needs a wife," he'd say, looking away from me and even though I never said nothing to that, I knew he was tilling the ground to ask me. I wasn't going to say nothing about it till he did, though.

The more we was together, the longer walks we'd take until one day we went past the strawberry fields and to the woods. We sat in the shade of a tired looking dogwood, swamped in the old thick humidity, and Ezra reached over and kissed me for the first time. He put his hand under my chin and lifted my head a little and kissed me, and I put my hand on his round shoulder.

"I love you, Clara."

"I love you, too," I said.

"I want us to be pleasing to the Lord."

"Oh, I want that too, Ezra," I told him, folding my hands in my lap.

"I want our love to be between God and me and you.

The three of us. I want the two of us to be in Christ and our union to be the mouth that speaks His message."

I smiled. "You're preaching, Ezra."

His face was scruffy because he hadn't shaved since Sunday, and he scratched the hairs on his chin. "I know," he said. "I don't mean to preach, Clara, but I want us to serve Him together."

"I do too," I told him.

That night, laying on the floor, I thought all about me and Ezra. I thought about being a preacher's wife. Margie said I wasn't married yet because I was too stubborn to let a man have me. I'd had my share of callers but Ezra, even though he was a boy, moved me more than the rest of them did. I thought about a lot of things that night and it got late—so late the grasshoppers outside were roaring at each other in their heat—and I thought about Ezra as a man. I was curled up against the wall, and I felt my breath on my face and imagined it was his, and I wanted to be with him right there.

And then I knew how evil I was. I knew that Ezra didn't want that and that he wanted us to glorify the Lord, and here I was thinking about wickedness. I crept up and past Margie snoring in the corner. I unlatched the door, closing it behind me and stood in the front yard. I looked up at the distant sky all dark blue around the moon and thought of my Jesus looking down on me, giving me the strength to hold on, promising me a good husband and children and a lifetime of service for His kingdom if I could just hold on. That sky was beautiful.

I looked down. The dirt was cool on my feet. Inching my toes down into it, I smiled at it.

* * *

"A man of God has got to stay clean before the Lord," Ezra would tell me with his blue eyes all sad and sweet at the same time.

"You are clean," I'd tell him, "and I want to be clean for you. I love you so much, and I want to be clean for you."

We had a hard time with that, and he prayed for us, and I told him I prayed for us, too, but I guess I lied about that. I tried to pray for us, but that'd only get me thinking about Ezra and me, and I'd think sinful thoughts right there in the middle of praying. I don't know where the evil come from to make me do that. I don't know if it was just me or if it was that natural evil that goes back to the Garden.

Ezra prayed for us, but I wasn't strong enough. I've thought a lot about it in sixty years, but I still ain't sure why I let it happen. One day we laid a blanket down out in the woods and it was like Ezra kissed me for the first time. We'd been holding and hugging and pecking before that, but that day he kissed me real and deep, and my old dark heart slowed down, like a water pump. I lost my breath and lay on my back and pulled him to me.

Even this afternoon, sitting in my chair with my hands folded on my Bible, I can feel his skin and muscles and smell the pine trees and the strawberries. The air was so thick it was like a damp sheet on our bodies. My ancient skin, eighty-five years old, still quivers a little at the thought. But, of course, the shame always comes with it, too.

I cried that first time because it hurt me. But Ezra cried, too, because he felt so bad about it. He stood up and stuck his hands in his pockets and looked through the leaves at the sky and prayed aloud for us while I cried and prayed and bled.

"Oh Mighty God, forgive us," he prayed. "Forgive me for this evil deed and for my damnable weakness." He squeezed his eyes shut and raised his hands and cried, "God damn this evil deed that we done! Purge us of this evil desire! Forgive us, we beg You, Jesus! We know You are an angry, vengeful God! Please! Please, dearest Jesus, forgive this woman for what she has done and purge her of these evil charms and purge me of my damnable weakness!" He was like that for a long time, standing on the blanket and yelling at the empty blue sky, while I lay by his feet and sobbed.

Laying on the floor that night, I prayed for forgiveness for what me and Ezra had done. I was hoping that Jesus was forgiving me for it as I prayed, but I wasn't sure, so I promised Him that I wouldn't do it again.

Ezra come to see me the next day, and Margie asked him to stay for lunch.

"No thank you," he said sticking his hands in his pockets. "I thought me and Clara might take a walk."

Margie smiled at me and said, "Why don't y'all take some biscuits with you? I'm gonna skin them rabbits the boys shot, and if y'all get back in time y'all can have some."

"Okay," I said, slipping on my shoes.

We walked down to the road and went across it to Mr. Anderson's field. We hadn't said nothing by the time we slipped through the barbwire and started across the field.

"Ezra," I said finally, "you mad at me?"

He was quiet and there was no sound but the dry

55

grass crunching beneath our shoes. It was windy that day, so I took a piece of yarn out of the pocket of my skirt and tied my long brown hair back into a ponytail. When we reached the trees he said, "What we done was evil, Clara. We knowed better than to do what we done. We both have the Spirit to hold us back, and He done His job, but it's me and you that sinned." Ezra's thick black hair was whipping around his head like a storm cloud and his face was pink.

I started to cry. We walked through the woods and after a little ways, the ground sloped down into a clearing of stumps, muddy tracks and some tore-up ground leading off onto a trail.

I sat down on the slope, and Ezra walked down into the clearing and looked around.

"This is where Mr. Anderson's new house is gonna be I reckon," Ezra said, not looking at me when he said it. "Must be nice to own land yourself."

I cried harder and I couldn't see nothing but the blurry ground, but I heard twigs snap and leaves crinkle, and Ezra put his arm around my shoulder. His hip was pressed next to mine.

"I still love you," he said.

"I'm dirty to you," I cried into my hands. "You ain't gonna want nothing to do with me."

"Did you pray through last night?" he asked. His voice was soft like he was kneeling at the altar with a sinner, trying to lead them to Jesus.

"Yes, I prayed all night." It wasn't strictly true, but I had prayed a lot.

"So did I," he said, "and He's faithful and just to forgive us, Clara."

I looked up at his smile and hugged his neck. "I

wanted to be pure for you, and I know you wanted me to be pure."

He put his arm around my waist and pulled me closer to him and kissed me. His eyes were closed hard, and he tried to gently lower me on the ground.

I pulled away a little. "Ezra, what are you doing?"

His smooth face was empty and he kissed my cheek. "Nothing," he said. "I love you. I want to kiss you is all."

I wanted to ask if that was all right, but I didn't. I nodded and said, "I want to kiss you, too."

But that wasn't all and after we lay down and kissed for a long time, he unbuttoned my blouse and lifted my skirt. When we were finished, he stood in the scarred clearing and prayed aloud again, begging forgiveness and screaming at the sky.

After that, I'd make him stay at Margie's with me, and we'd sit there and talk about the crop we'd brought in or about church.

Sometimes though, Ezra would get me out to the woods on a walk, or even, once, on the way home from church and we'd lay in the leaves and make love and then, most of the times, I'd cry and he'd pray. Sometimes when he prayed, he'd pray so hard that he'd weep himself.

Then, not too long after we had the crop in, I realized that I was pregnant. Margie had told me all about it when I had my first lady's time, and when I started missing, I knew what I'd done. I ran out to the bare strawberry fields and wailed like I was gone mad. I kicked the dirt and ripped one of the wooden row markers out of the ground and flung it as hard as I could. Cursing my body for its wickedness, I fell to the ground.

Then Margie was beside me.

I looked up at her, and she seemed to fill the sky. Her back was to the sun, and its light spread out behind her, darkening her face. Strands of her hair whipped at her rough cheeks as she said, "You're gonna have a child, ain't you?"

I looked at the dirt.

"Stop crying, girl. Does Ezra know?"

I shook my head.

"Then you need to get up and go tell him. Come on, stand up."

I climbed up and looked at her. I realized that I was a little taller than she was. Her thick jaw jerked from side to side as she ground her gums together and wrinkles spread out from her chin like spider webs.

"You're mad at me," I said.

"I'm ashamed of you. I never wanted no girl because I always knowed I'd do a poor job raising one. You knowed better than to do this to yourself. Men ain't got the same good sense as a woman. That's all you got on a man in this world. They're bigger and stronger and they run things, but the last man with any kind of good sense was Jesus Christ Hisself."

"I done lost that, I reckon."

"Get it back then. The Lord didn't hang on that cross for nothing. You got the free will He give us all, and you got to throw yourself on Him, cause only He's going to see you through. You do that on your way to tell that boy you're gonna have his child. You throw yourself back to Jesus."

I wiped my face and leaned over. I put my arms around her, but she stood there like she was made of rock.

When I let go of her, she nodded toward the road. "You best go tell Ezra what y'all done to yourselves."

I found him behind the church, where the woods came up to the edge of the yard and the children had their Sunday School. He was chopping down a tree, and there was already a pile of wood in a big square wheelbarrow beside him.

"Howdy, Ezra," I said behind him.

He turned and smiled at me. "Hey there, Clara, what are you doing?"

"Just coming to see you."

He sunk the ax into the tree and left it stuck there while he told me, "I'm chopping wood for the pastor. He says it's gonna be snow early this year on account of the leaves turning so quick. That new stove we got for the church can hold more wood than I ever seen..." He stopped and looked at me, and said, "What's wrong, Clara?"

"I'm gonna have your child," I said.

He didn't do nothing. He just stood there without even his face changing. Just looked at me like he was still waiting for an answer to his question.

It was getting cold, but he was sweating from his work. He reached up and ran his thumbnail across his eyebrows, and sweat dripped off his hand.

"Are you sure?"

"Yes."

His Adam's apple jerked out from his throat like he was swallowing something big, and he looked down at his hands. I watched him and thought how his hands was just skin and muscle and bone like ever one else's.

Spinning around, he jerked the ax out of the tree and then slammed it back and the tree shook and scarlet leaves sparkled down on him like fire from the sky. He flung the ax head at the tree again, but he was too mad and he missed it and snapped the handle in two. Throwing the handle away, he started beating the tree with his hands till he was out of breath and his fists was red.

"What are you gonna do?" I whispered, moving behind the wheelbarrow.

He leaned against the scarred up tree and said, "I'm gonna marry you."

We got married a week later and got a little place joining onto Margie's. We all made a deal with Mr. Anderson that we'd work both tracts with Margie's family, but he'd pay us like we was each working our own land separate.

Since our house was close to the water, it was built off the ground and had a wide, railless front porch. Margie had never wanted that house, even though it was a bit better, because she said that when the floods came it wouldn't matter that the house was a few feet off the ground because it would flood anyhow. Still though, I was happy about getting a place for me and Ezra.

Something bad fell over him after we got married, though. He didn't touch me much. I reckoned I didn't attract him on account of being pregnant, but he didn't even kiss me good night nor hold my hand in church.

He didn't speak in church no more after we got married, neither. There was about thirty of us in the congregation, and we'd sing, and the preacher would ask someone to testify, and where once old Ezra would have shot up and preached, now he just sat there looking down at his hands, mumbling a prayer.

He'd sit out on our porch in the morning and read his Bible and pray. One morning, because he was praying so loud, I woke up. Laying there I listened:

"Oh God, I'm Your servant. Forgive me. Forgive me. Burn this flesh away till there is only a soul. Only a soul that longs for You."

I laid there and closed my eyes and shut his voice out. Rubbing my stomach I smiled because I could feel the little body inside me, pressing against my flesh and breathing the fluids in my body. My back ached something terrible, but the pain was warm and the ache in my swelled breasts made me cup them gently and imagine the child in me feeding from them one day.

Outside Ezra moaned louder:

"Please, please, please. Burn away this evil flesh. Hurry that day when it is no more and there is only a soul. Only a soul in love with You."

The creek lowered and froze up not long after that, and we had to break through the ice with hammers and haul the water up to the house in buckets. It'd freeze up overnight, and the next morning we'd have to break it up again.

One morning, Ezra woke me up. He was standing there nudging the bed with his foot. "Hey. Hey, Clara."

"Yeah," I said, opening my eyes as the bed shook.

"C'mon and get your clothes on and help me get some water."

I got up and slipped on a thick coat and some wool leg warmers Margie made me. I pulled on my boots, and we walked outside. The sun was just a white smear in a sky that was just a bigger gray smear, and I was freezing the second we got out there. Ezra got the hammer and handed me one of the buckets, and we started for the creek. The ground was froze hard and it felt like we was walking on iron.

"I'm gonna go get us some wood before breakfast," he said.

"We got some of them eggs left, and I'll mix you biscuits to take with you if you want."

"I'll eat em when I get back," he said. "I ain't got time to wait for em."

The tree limbs along the way was stripped bare and a sharp wind blew through them and seemed to peel your skin off. I was shuddering by the time we got down to the muddy creek, which was froze so hard you could mistake it for rock. A few dead weeds around the bank stuck out of the brown ice like hairs on a man's chin. Ezra leaned down at the bank and took a couple of hard whacks at the ice.

"Son of a bitch," he cussed.

I never heard him cuss before. I couldn't believe he said that, but I didn't want to say nothing about it. I asked, "Is it harder than yesterday?"

"What do you think?" He hit it again a couple of times and cussed again. "Damn water," he said and threw the hammer at it. "Damn water," he yelled stomping on the ice. He tried for the hammer but slipped on the ice and come down heavy on his knee. He grabbed the hammer and scrambled to the bank. He let out a scream like I never heard come out of any man before or since. He beat the ice and sharp chips of it flew up. "Damn this ice," he yelled. "Damn this world!" Standing up, he struck himself in the same leg he fell on and he grunted curses at his own body.

"Ezra," I yelled.

I grabbed his arm, and he shoved me to the ground. I fell on my side and he come toward me. I covered my stomach. "Damn that wicked flesh," he grunted. "That filthy growth ruint me."

"Please, Jesus," I prayed. "Please, Jesus. I call on Your holy name, Jesus."

I wasn't crying. My head was down, and my eyes were closed and when I looked up, he was gone. I climbed up and rubbed my stomach.

I started back home. He hates my flesh and his own, but he still loves me, I told myself. He just hates our evil old flesh. It was only calling on the name of Jesus that stopped Ezra from hurting me.

The thought come to me that the Spirit had stopped the flesh.

I got to the house and went inside. Ezra was gone to cut the wood, and I sat down on our bed. I knew I needed to get up and fix him some breakfast, but I got to thinking about how I was eating more than before, feeding my growth.

I've thought a lot about what was going through my head that morning. I was crazy with fear and sadness. I told myself how I wouldn't have to eat so much and how I could work more, but none of that was really why.

I loved my body. I loved the ways it was changing and the little legs and arms stretching in my belly. I loved everything good and bad about it. And, I figured, that was my sin. It was ruining Ezra and it was ruining me. We both wanted to be closer to God, and my evil old body was a ugly thing sitting in our path.

I walked outside and the air stung my face. The fields were gray with a hard solid frost. I looked down from the porch at the iron ground. I didn't cry. Looking up at the gray sky I took a deep breath, spread my arms, and fell forward.

Falling, the ground flying up at me, I knew in a instant that it was wrong. But the ground crashed into me like a train, and my nose shattered and my arm snapped back. My stomach felt like a crushed grape. Warm blood spilled onto the frozen ground, and I wept.

He put me in bed and ran and brought the doctor, and the doctor told him the baby was dead. After the doctor and his nurse had operated on me, cleaned up and gone, I lay on the bed with my face to the wall.

"Clara," he said.

"Clara," he said again, even softer. He sat down on the bed, but he didn't touch me.

I could feel where the little body had been, and I was still crying, holding my stomach.

"Clara, he's with Jesus now."

"It was a boy?"

"Yes."

That made me cry a little. I told him, "I wish I was dead, too, so I could be with him. So I could be with my little baby and not with you."

I was looking at the plank in the wall. He didn't say nothing for a long time and then all he said was my name.

I told him, "I hate you. I hate you and I'm gonna hate you all my life. The only feelings I got left in this world is my love for that baby and my hate for you."

He sat there for a long time and then the mattress shook as he got up. He blew out the lamp and left. It was dark in the room cause the sun hadn't come out in days and the moon hadn't risen yet.

I lay there a long time knowing my little baby would never be a little boy and would never grow up to be a man. And I knew Ezra wasn't coming back. Poor Ezra. Only the Lord Himself knows how empty Ezra must have felt. I cried for him, and for me, and for the baby.

After a while, the door opened, and a little light come in from the moon. I didn't want it to be Ezra. I didn't want him near me.

Then Margie touched my arm. Her fingertips were cold at first but then became warm and being touched that softly by another human being was like being touched by Jesus Himself.

"Come here, child," she whispered.

I rolled over to her, and she held me in the dark; her hands and arms and breath like the Spirit of God made real, just to hold me.

COLD CITY

Graham said he needed to talk. I had to go outside for a cigarette break anyway, so we walked downstairs. Wet snow flurries pelted the sidewalks, and all the smokers wedged into a space just beside the front door to keep out of the wind. Graham motioned me away from the smoker's nook, though. What he had to say was private. He didn't want to say it around a bunch of cops.

We dashed across the street to a greasy spoon where most of us ate before or after our shifts. We took a booth in the back and ordered a couple of coffees. I lit up a cigarette and said, "Let's have it."

"I'm in trouble, Larry. I'm in a damn mess."

Graham scratched his smooth forehead. Even when I was a rookie I looked about fifty. That's a good quality for a cop to have. Graham was thirty years old, but he looked all of twenty-one.

"Tell me," I said.

He nodded and took a sip of his coffee. He sucked in his upper lip a little and put down the cup. "It's money. I'm in debt way over my head. It's going to break me if I don't do something soon. Real soon."

"How much?"

"Thirty grand."

"Jesus."

He nodded. "Yeah."

"I take it we're not talking about student loans here."

He took a deep breath. "No. Dirt Bramson."

"Damn, kid." I sat there smoking for a moment. He stared down at his hands. Finally, I said, "Three things you can do on a deal like this. One, you go talk to him and try to get an extension."

"I tried, but—"

"Just shut up," I snapped. "Just sit there and listen to me. You can go talk to him and try to get an extension, but Dirt's a grade A asshole. Plus, he hates cops. He'd probably love to send someone around to break your knees. Or he might just let it leak to the guys upstairs that you're into him for thirty g's. So option one is out. Option two, you can try to raise the money some other way."

"How do I get my hands on that kind of cash?"

I looked him straight in the eye and shrugged. "Depends on what you want to do."

"Okay," he said. "What's option three?"

I mashed out my butt and leaned forward. "You get rid of him."

Graham ran his hand over his face. I'd never stared at him before—not really. I'd never noticed that he was kind of delicate looking. Odd for a cop. He was a good kid, good at his job, though. He had a deep, authoritative voice, and he didn't take any shit from smart-mouthed dickheads, but if you just saw him walking around on the street you'd swear he was a high school math teacher.

"Yeah," he said.

I stirred some sugar into my coffee and took a sip. I

added more sugar.

"What would you do, Larry?"

I sighed. "Tough to know what to do."

He let out a curt chuckle and shook his head in disgust. "I can't believe I got myself into this. This wasn't how the old man raised me."

Graham had a daddy complex. His old man had been some kind of preacher, and the kid always beat himself up because he wasn't John the Baptist.

He ran his hands over his face. "It shouldn't be tough to know what to do."

What can you say to that? If God wanted us to have moral clarity he shouldn't have created us blind and stupid.

I pushed away my coffee and stood up. "You'll figure something out, kid. Do what you got to do. What's more important, you or Dirt?"

I left him sitting there and ran back over to the station. We didn't talk the rest of the day, but that night I followed him home. He lived in a little brownstone not far away, and I tailed him in the snow. He went inside about seven.

I parked my car down the street and sat. I smoked up the last of my pack. I had some coffee from my old green thermos.

I'd had the thermos ten years. Mom got it for me for Christmas the year before she died.

"You need warm coffee on a chilly stakeout," she'd said.

When she said it, she probably didn't have this particular stakeout in mind.

The kid came out of his house at about ten and climbed in his car. I trailed him at a close distance. The snow provided good cover, and I could afford to stick closer than I usually would.

We rode across town and the kid parked a few blocks away from Dirt's joint. It was the back room of a cigarette store. The store was owned by Dirt's old man, a fat redneck from way down south who had a thick Mississippi accent and always acted as if he had no idea what his son did for a living. He closed up shop about six every day and left the back door open.

I followed the kid with snow-heavy winds slapping us the whole way. I expected Graham to turn into the alley that led behind the store, but instead he walked to the front door. The place had once had a heavy gate, but some drunk had run her car into it a few months before and the old man hadn't replaced it yet. Graham looked around, and not seeing anyone, he crouched down and picked the lock on the front door. It took him a while, but he got it open and went inside.

I crept up to the window and saw him go behind the counter. The old man had a piece back there. Graham found it, checked it and came back around. I hustled back to my hiding place and watched him come out. He braced himself against the wind and headed down the alley.

Why not just sneak in through the store? I wondered. Maybe he wanted to scope out the place first and make sure Dirt was alone.

I stomped my feet to get some feeling back into my toes, and I waited. I looked down the street.

Wet clumps of snow splattered on the sidewalk, while overhead, dirty gray clouds floated across the moon like ice drifts. Down the street I heard the damp crunch of tires.

Headlights split the darkness and glittered off the snow in front of me. I sunk deeper into my little nook as the car got closer, sloshing through the streams of ice and water. I lost my breath when I realized it was a patrol car.

Two man team. I could barely make them out. Gutierrez and Parker.

Shit.

Gutierrez was driving. He slowed to a halt in front of the cigarette store.

The sky spit snow, and the car idled in front of the store. I waited for the gun shot.

Gutierrez and Parker were talking. They seemed intent on whatever it was they were discussing. Then Parker leaned over and kissed Gutierrez. At first, Gutierrez didn't move, but then he put his hand on Parker's shoulder and pulled him closer.

They were still making out when the gun shot exploded from the cigar shop.

The boys looked toward the store, and Parker said something. Gutierrez threw the car into drive and they pulled away but not too fast, not too harried. The car crawled to the end of the street, its taillights bleeding over the ice and slush, and at the stop sign, it turned and disappeared.

Less than a minute later, Graham ran out of the alley. He slipped and fell in some snow, picked himself up and bolted down the street.

I didn't waste time. He was barely gone before I ran across the street and down the alley. I drew my gun as I got to the back door of the cigarette store. The door was cracked, and I nudged it opened and pushed through the curtain. Dirt lay on the floor in a widening pool of blood, a single shot in the head.

71

If I knew Graham like I thought I did, he wouldn't have checked Dirt for the book. Sure enough, it was there, tucked in his back pocket.

I pulled it out, shoved it in my coat and got the hell out of there.

Two days later he came to my desk and sat down. I was eating a Pop Tart and having some coffee.

Graham looked thin and ashen, but his blue eyes were lit up like a neon sign.

"You hear about Dirt Bramson?" he asked.

"Yeah. Not a big blow to humanity."

"Culliton and Varner are working the case."

"Good men," I said. I dipped some Pop Tart in my coffee and ate it. That made the Pop Tart even better, if such a thing were possible. "Still, they have bigger fish to fry than Dirt. Everybody in town wanted to kill that hillbilly."

The kid nodded. "I hear Dirt's book is missing."

I sipped some coffee and looked at him.

He asked, "You hear the same thing?"

"Unsubstantiated rumor."

"Yeah? It struck me as being the kind of thing someone would do for a reason."

"Like what?" I asked.

"Like if they were in the book. They'd kill Dirt and then take the book." He looked around and then leaned in. "Or they might forget the book and then someone else, say someone else who was also in there, he might come along and take it."

"Well, kid," I said, "I guess that's possible. Either way, I'm sure whoever took it disposed of it promptly.

Like I said, everyone in town wanted to kill that asshole."

Graham shook his head and leaned back in his chair. "It doesn't make murder right."

"Nope," I said standing up. "But we have other crimes to investigate. You gotta make a hierarchy of what you're going to care about. The murder of Dirt Bramson is pretty low down everybody's list."

"And that's all there is?" he said.

"What else could there be?"

He closed his eyes. "God?"

I threw my coffee cup in the trash. "Just another unsubstantiated rumor."

MICROECONOMICS

That meth head got a garbage bag. All the shit she could have drug in here, she drug in a goddamn garbage bag.

A white man comes up to the counter. "Miss, do you see that woman over in the corner?"

I look up at the clock. Not even ten minutes 'til we close. Davon supposed to be here exactly at eleven. I know him, he ain't gonna show up a minute early.

The white man got a pink face and a white mustache. He leans over the register and stares over his glasses like his face gonna scare me. He say each word real slow like I got a learning disability. "Excuse me. Miss. Do you see that woman?"

"Yeah."

"Well, do you happen to see that she's rummaging through a trash sack?"

I look over at the meth head. She sitting at a table by the door that goes out to the playground. She got the big black bag at her feet and she digging through it. She mumbling something to herself. Sound like, "Do you mind?"

I just kind of sigh and look at the clock again. It ain't hardly moved at all.

The white man goes, "There a manager on duty?"

"Me."

"Well, then, I think you should probably go do something about that. I'm sure the McDonald's corporation would be interested to know that you stood here while some woman dug through an industrial-sized garbage bag in the dining room of their restaurant."

I look for Jaylen. He over by the bathroom with the mop bucket. He looking at the meth head, too, but he ain't gonna do nothing. He just standing there, skinny as that mop handle, tugging at the belt on his pants. He so skinny he had to poke new holes in the belt with a screwdriver. He just looking at the meth head, tugging his belt like a damn kid. He ain't going to do nothing. That man worthless.

I come around the counter.

The white man goes, "Well, finally." He got on khaki cargo shorts and a blue polo shirt. Got his fists on his hips like he Superman.

I walk over to the meth head. There ain't nobody left in the place except me, Jaylen, the white man, and her. I say, "Hey, you can't do that in here. You gots to go."

She got hair like rust—orange and dry and dead. Her face white like a piece of chalk but she got bloody sores all around her mouth. She say, "Do you mind?"

"Yeah, I do. You gots to go."

"Do you mind? Do you mind? Do you mind?"

"Lady, you needs to go. We gots to close. You can't have no trash bag in here."

"Do you mind? Do you mind? Do you mind?" She goes back to digging in her sack of trash. "Do you mind?"

I ain't got but a few minutes to get her out the door before Davon comes rolling up. I reach down and pull at her garbage sack. It heavy and wet and smells like shit. The meth head yanks back on it and she look up at me with eyes so wild ass blue it's like they shove me away. Even with all the drugs this woman ever done, her eyes still blue as tinted contacts.

"Do you mind? Do you mind?"

I pull at the sack and she pulls back and I say real loud, "You best let go of this sack!"

She lets go.

I drag the sack to the front door, leaking disgusting garbage all the way across the floor. I open the front door and push it out onto the curb of the parking lot.

I go back over to the meth head. "Get up. We closed. You gots to go."

She mumbling to herself, "Do you mind? Do you mind? Do you mind?" She stands up. "Do you mind? Do you mind?"

I take her to the front door. She walks through the garbage water. I open the front door. She goes out there and picks up her garbage sack. "Do you mind?"

I close the door.

Jaylen goes, "She crazy out of her mind."

I point my thumb at the garbage water. "Since you ain't help me get her out the door and since you leaning on that mop, how about you mop that shit up?"

Any minute now Davon gonna come rolling up. I gots to go make sure the door to the manager's office is open so it makes it look like I just unlocked it when the robber breaks in. I ain't got to worry none about the safe, though. It busted last night and can't close proper. They supposed to have sent someone out here today to fix it, but ain't nobody showed up. So all I gots to do is make sure that the manager's office open so Davon can pop in and out.

Then I see the white man. He still there, hands on his hips, looking at me.

He unclips the cell phone on his belt. He goes, "Ma'am, may I have your name?"

"Tameka," I say. I look at the clock. Ten fifty-eight.

He open up his phone. He making a note. He gonna rat me out to McDonald's. He can't spell my name, though. He tap in the T but then he looks at me and goes, "How do you spell that?"

I stare at him. I ain't a violent person. I been around enough bad shit that I could be. But I ain't. Just ain't me. But I want to kill this man. I do. I really would like to kill him.

Ten fifty-nine.

"T-A-M-E-K-A. My last name Jones. J-O-N-E-S."

"I know how to spell Jones," he say while he tapping his phone. "That's my last name."

"Sir, we closed now. You gots to go."

"Fine. I just want you to know that I will be reporting this to—"

He stops. He looking over my shoulder. I turn around and sees Davon coming through the door with a Walmart bag on his head. He got it taped together at the bottom to keep it on and got two holes poked through for his eyes. He got the gun in his hand.

The white man don't say nothing, he just turns around and runs out the other door.

Davon yells "Hey" at him but the white man gone.

Now Davon points the gun between me and Jaylen. "Get yo ass over there" he say and Jaylen drops his mop and hurries over to the counter by me. Fastest I ever seen him move. "Get that office open," Davon say. "Quick now."

He say that "Quick now" for me, because that white man that run out of here probably already on the phone to the police. They probably already on the way.

I run over to the office and pull out the keys from my pocket and there's a terrible sound like a explosion like two three four explosions and I jump up and drop the keys. Davon pull the trigger by accident? But I turn around and Davon on the floor and blood coming out of him.

The white man standing in the door, gun in his hand. Jaylen standing by the counter with Davon's blood on his face.

The white man, "Are y'all okay?"

Jaylen, feeling hisself, looking for holes. "Yeah. Yeah." He look at me. "Tameka, you okay?"

Davon ain't breathing. The plastic is stuck to his face, and I can see it ain't moving.

"Tameka, you okay?"

The white man on his phone, tapping 911. "Yes. There's been a shooting. At McDonald's over on Eugene Road. A robbery. I shot a man with a gun. Black male, maybe twenty-five years old. Hard to tell because he's got a mask on. He broke in here and tried to rob the place. He had a gun. My name is—"

I walk over to Davon.

White man goes, "Miss? What are you doing, miss?"

"Tameka, what you doing?"

"Miss?"

I pull the gun out of Davon's hand.

No more. No more of this.

GOOD COVER

For an hour, I've been crouched beside this half-opened window with my eye sweating against my rifle scope. I try not to think about the time, try not to think about this long hour I've been waiting for someone to walk out the front door of the office building across the street.

It's best not to wait. It's best to clear your mind. Your mind doesn't need to exist for this kind of deal, anyway. All you need is one eye and a trigger finger.

I've been shooting people since I was a kid. I shot my first human being on a snowy Monday night in downtown Cleveland. Some businessman hailing a cab. I leaned out a window facing an alley and blew his skull to pieces with one shot to the forehead. I left Cleveland that night. A year later, I shot a pregnant woman sitting on a park bench fanning herself on a warm Sunday morning in Dallas. Two for one. I went on a bit of a spree after that.

But I was just a wild ass kid those days. I'm sane enough to know that serial killers all end up getting caught at some poi—

The guy comes out, clutching the hair of a screaming little girl in one hand, an old revolver in the other. He's shouting threats when I pull the trigger and split his head like a piñata. Blood, bone, and brain spray the glass door of the office building while his body, seized by gravity now, thuds to the ground.

The little girl wails. Her mother runs up to her, thanking god, surrounded by fifty cops. One of them turns around and gives me the thumbs up.

"Bad guy down," someone crackles into my earpiece. "Nice shooting."

I'm a hero again.

THE SERPENT BOX

As he took the bible from his nightstand, Tore King called across the hall to his daughter and told her to wake up. She did not answer him back, and he heard no indication of her stirring as he passed her closed door on his way into the den. Small spikes of ice hung from one of the logs in the wall where rain had seeped in during the night. King broke the ice down into a pot and placed it on the warm black stove in the center of the room.

"Karen," he called, "I said to get up. I ain't going to meeting this morning, so you're gonna have to take the serpents early."

After a moment, her voice drifted back, "I'm awake, Daddy," and he heard the first faint rustlings of her sheets. He dipped a cloth into the pot and washed his lean face and neck. Then he wrapped the cloth around the handle and took the steaming water to her thin, wooden door and knocked.

When it opened, the girl was still in her white night-gown. Though she was fifteen, she looked no more than twelve. Her face was round, with ruddy cheeks and a thick ball of a nose. "You ain't going to meeting?" she asked, taking the handle from him.

"Got rained out yesterday," he reminded her. "The

mill's been setting idle two days now. I reckon my ox is in a ditch." He turned and started down the hall. "You need to get moving. I had enough of your sleeping."

She nodded and closed the door, and he walked over to his reading table. He was sitting there with his bible when she came out, still in her nightgown, and warmed herself by the stove. Pressing his reading glasses to his thin, skin-flaked lips, he watched her and thought of whipping her for slothfulness. He decided not to. It was Sabbath morning, and he did not want to begin it with a beating.

"I spect they're gonna be needing the serpents down there before noonday," he said. "Brother Hiram asked us special to get them there early."

"Brother Hiram," the girl sneered. "I don't know why you pay that man no mind at all after the way he done Momma."

King stood and walked over to the stove to warm his hands. "Best be watching your tongue, girl," he said. "He's still the shepherd of our flock."

"That shepherd," she said, "told everyone Momma died on account of her not having enough faith. Momma! You know that ain't the truth, but you let him say it."

"Girl!" he shouted, jerking toward her, his narrow face tilting in so that the cold blue of his eyes seemed to jump at her. Shrinking away from him, she tightened her muscles, ready to absorb a physical reprimand, but he steadied himself, rocking on the heels of his work-boots, his long, thick hands still at his sides.

"I'm sorry, Daddy," she said, her back touching the cold logs in the wall.

"Just hush," he said, squeezing his eyes shut. "Just hush. Now listen. The preacher's a good man of God.

He may not a been right about Momma, but that ain't for us to handle. We got to handle our own faith and for us the believing is in the forgiving. I forgive him even if he's wrong. That's the whole thing. Your momma was as good a woman of the Lord ever walked this earth. She's with Him now. You just keep that in mind, and remember that she'd have you forgive Brother Hiram." His eyes opened and he regarded her a moment. "You just never need to forget that in the eyes of Jesus, we're all of us sinners."

After a quick breakfast of biscuits and coffee, King walked out to the wooden shed behind the house. It was sturdy and well insulated, and stood between the house and the horse barn. In the floor of the shed were two small doors, which King pulled open. He drew out two finely crafted, stained-oak boxes. On the lid of each box shone a brass handle and latch and the inscription: Mark 16:15-18. King carried the boxes to the barn and saddled the girl's horse, clamping each box into a special iron rigging on the saddle.

A slow, heavy thunder tumbled over the dampened mountains. When the girl came outside she wore a maroon dress and a thin, emerald jacket her mother had made for her. In the bruised sky above her, a white mist twisted and unfurled like a banner on the breeze.

"You go get your heavy coat, girl."

"This one's pretty, Daddy."

Her father grunted. "You go get that coat fore I whip you. I can't make you wear it, but it ain't a bad idea to have it along."

The girl shrugged and loped back inside. King surveyed the sky again. Around the darkened edges of the trees the sky was starting to turn pink, and the moon was evaporating into the mist. When the girl came back outside she was smiling, still wearing the emerald jacket but carrying a thick brown coat.

"What're you grinning like a possum at?"

"I'm just happy," she said. "It's Sabbath day, and I ain't got to help at the sawmill none."

He shook his head. "That all Sabbath day is to you? A reason not to work?"

She climbed onto the horse and straightened her skirt. "No, Daddy. It's a opportunity to forgive Brother Hiram his trespasses."

He pulled his long, callous fingers across his scalp of graying-blond hair. "I can't believe I raised such a blaspheming girl."

"I'm sorry, Daddy," she said. "I'll be good." She leaned down, a wisp of her long blonde hair floating beneath her chin, and stuck out her lips for a kiss.

He kissed her. "I won't be at meeting tonight, neither," he said. "I got to finish working that back acre. You come on home tomorrow morning if Sister Barris will put you up tonight. If she don't, you just head on home after dinner this afternoon."

"Yes, Daddy," she said.

King watched his daughter ride away. He feared that he detected the first scent of a hard rain.

Halfway between her cabin and the church, the girl met two strangers on the road. One was thin shouldered and bearded. He wore a floppy gray hat and when he smiled at her and said, "Howdy, sweet miss," she saw that he had only a few blackened teeth left in his mouth.

She nodded and said, "Howdy," clutching the horse's rein. On the wooded ridge just above her, a heavy fog hung in the trees like a drawn curtain, and the fat croaks of unseen toads echoed down the slope.

The other stranger was a shivering boy not much older than Karen herself. He had many teeth, big and jumbled in his mouth, so that when he smiled they almost seemed to spill out. The boy held an old, skinny goat by a frayed rope.

"Would you like to buy that goat there, miss?" the man asked her. "We ain't got no food, nor no money for food. Ain't even got a gun to shoot us a squirrel with. Just this here goat, and we ain't got the heart to kill him for eating." He glanced back at the boy. The shaking youth rubbed his yellowed palms together, staring at Karen with a dull smile drifting across his lips like an afterthought. "Don't mind him," the man told her. "He can't talk. Not a word."

"I'm sorry," she said. "I don't have no money. I'm heading to the church house, and I need to be hurrying." She wanted to get past the men now that she knew they were hungry, because she feared they would steal the horse, or her coat, and sell them. She had heard of such things.

"Ain't going to put no money in the plate this morning?" the man asked.

"I reckon not today," she said. In a small, white purse tied to her belt beneath the coat she had a dollar that she intended to give to the church as an offering. She thought about giving it to the man, but she didn't want the folks at church to think she was too stingy to tithe. "If y'all want to come with me, I reckon you'd get some dinner after meeting."

"That's mighty sweet," the man said. He smiled again, and the pointed, red cheeks above his beard nearly obscured his eyes in crinkled flesh. He walked over and stroked the horse's neck, and as he did, his narrow chest touched the white lace hem of her dress. "What kind of church are you?"

His proximity sent a chill down her back. It was new to her, a different fear than ever fallen on her before. Her skin felt heavy and thick, like another coat the man might want to steal.

"Holiness," she said. "We're Holiness."

The man smiled even wider. "You all are snake handlers, ain't you?"

"Yes sir," she said. She motioned back at the boxes. "I'm taking the serpents up to the church house. My daddy's an elder and we keep the serpents for the church."

"I'd sure like to see them snakes," he said.

"Well," the girl said, "I got to take them to meeting. I'm already late."

"No," the man said. "No. You'll be there. Ain't it your duty to show us them snakes? I reckon I seen plenty, but I ain't never seen no snake handler's snakes."

"Just serpents," the girl said, her voice almost obscured by the croaking toads. "Copperheads."

"Copperheads! Y'all handle copperheads!"

Karen smiled. "Scripture says, them with faith shall pick up serpents and not be hurt."

The man grinned at the boy and said, "She's quoting scripture at us now."

The girl looked up at the mud-red sky through rattling tree limbs. "My daddy says that when you hold the serpent you're holding your faith in your own hand.

That's when you feel the Lord. My momma had faith," she said. "She did. She handled serpents most her life." She shook her head. "But one bit her a year ago. The preacher said that if she'd had enough faith she would of not died." She shook her head again. "My momma had faith."

"You got faith?" the man asked, lightly touching the silent box.

Karen's face was dry and the veins at the bridge of her nose were pale green. Her cheeks were almost purple with the assault of the constant, icy wind, and when she frowned at him, she looked as if she were in pain. "I got faith," she said. "I never handled them before, but I got faith." She stared at the man's sneer and said again, "I got faith."

She climbed down from the horse and began to wrestle one of the boxes out of its rigging. Walking around the horse, the boy watched her, his mouth hanging open.

The girl laid the box on the ground and knelt by it. She touched the lid's simple, cold latch. Kneeling in the man's tilting gray shadow, she stared down at the box.

"Are you ready?" she asked, and he grabbed her hair and flung her backwards into the mud. The horse jumped and started to gallop down the trail. "Get it!" the man yelled at the boy. Karen scrambled to her feet and lunged toward the woods. The man grabbed her muddied, emerald coat, and she turned and struck him in the mouth. Her face was tight and hard now, and he punched her, but she was free from him and was already to her feet.

He clutched his face, yelling, "Get the horse!" but the boy stood there dumbly, the goat kicking at his feet. The man turned and ran after her.

He caught her beneath a bare birch tree and threw her to the ground, and she cried out, "In the beginning was the Word and the Word was with God and the Word was God! In the beginning was the Word…"

He pinned her knees to the ground with his own and grasped under her dress, tearing away her undergarment. She screamed as if he had torn away a piece of her flesh. The boy was beside them, rubbing his hands for warmth, his mouth hanging open and silent. Karen called out, "The Word was with God and the Word was God!"

"Well, hold her hands," the man grunted. The boy reached down and took her wrists. As Karen thrashed about beneath him, the man picked up a smooth rock near his feet and struck her face with it.

Wet, steady winds shook the bending pines, and droplets of rain sprayed the two killers like pellets of bird shot. The man sat down, looking away from the body. "Now let me figure," he said. He rubbed his mouth; a quiet ache had begun where the girl struck him. He looked up at the boy, who stared at the body. "That horse is gone to hell and back. No use a-looking for it anyhow on account of it's probably lost in the woods where the trail goes thin."

The boy watched gray, dappled sunlight fall on the girl and shine in the tiny bubbles of rain on her cheeks. He walked over to her and bent down. The man turned and struck him in the thigh and the boy slithered away. The goat jumped with him and fell into a pile of wet leaves.

"You keep away from her," the man said. "You ain't

got to spoil her too." He turned away, looking up into the pines and trying to catch some light on his face. A hard wind slapped the tree tops and rain fell on him "Well," he said, hanging his head and rubbing the back of his long neck, "we got a coat for you, I reckon."

The boy shook his head.

The man peered up at him. "You ain't telling me you ain't gonna to wear it on account of it's a girl's?"

The boy had not stopped shaking his head.

"God damn you," the man said. "It's a good coat. If it'd fit me, I'd by God wear it."

The boy was still shaking his head.

The man shrugged. "Well, I ain't gonna make you wear it if you're set again it, but you're a goddamn fool if ever I saw one. Gonna freeze your ass when that rain comes back."

The boy smiled. The man shook his head again. "Goddamn fool," he said.

They walked back up to the muddy trail and glared at the snake box. "Snake handlers," the man said. "There's some crazy sons of bitches, I'll tell you what."

The boy nudged the box with his toe and squinted at the man.

"Oh yeah," the man said, "there's a snake in there, all right. I'll bet you she's a copperhead, too. Crazy. Them snake handlers is crazy in the head."

The box thumped and the boy jumped back. Shaking with laughter, the man slapped the boy on the back. "Well, go in and get her, Ignorant," he said. He straightened and laughed under his breath. "Oo-ee. Ignorant, I don't know what kind of man thinks he's gotta pick up a damn snake to feel the Lord, but you ain't that kind."

The boy jerked his head toward the box, his face red

and drawn. He waved his hand at it.

"No," the man said. "I don't reckon I'm that kind neither. I heard of specters chasing after folks. And the devil coming after you. But I don't reckon I seen nothing to make me believe in a good ghost, holy or no."

Thunder broke through the trees, and shadows swayed over the two like black flames. "We got to get out of this here rain," the man said. He started down the trail and then turned back to the boy. "You go fetch that coat. We can trade it on down the road for a boy's."

To this suggestion, the boy nodded in happy agreement.

When Tore King opened his door to the two strangers, he yelled over the storm, "Y'all come in out of that rain!" and the two dashed inside, the boy pulling the goat along. Shaking the rain off, the goat sprayed them all. Tore glared down at it.

"I'm sorry," the man said, leaning over and kicking the goat in the ribs. "Damn thing."

King shook his head. "When the rain lets up a little, one of y'all can take him out to the barn." He sat down in front of the stove, and the other two sat on a narrow bench on the opposite side. "What a day," King said. He poured some coffee and passed the man a steaming cup. "Where abouts are y'all from?"

"Down round Black Tree," the man said. "Just come out of Missouri and heading on through. I don't reckon to be in Arkansas much longer."

King nodded. "Y'all are welcome to stay the night. I figure it'll be a cold one tonight." He stopped and looked at the boy. "You don't say much."

"Ah, sir," the man said, "he can't talk. On account of no tongue. He's born without one. You ever hear of such a thing? I been doing all his talking for him most his life."

"That's a mighty heavy cross to bear," King said. "Don't reckon I'd want that position."

The man nodded and ran the back of his thin, hairy hand over his face, wiping off the rain. "Well, sir, it ain't easy, you know. It ain't. I done the best I could, though. Ignorant here's like a brother to me. He is. And I tried to do right by him." He scratched his head. "Ain't always succeeded. Got him off track a time or two, I reckon."

"How'd you go about that?"

The man shrugged. "Oh, getting him into all sort of wickedness with me." The man looked into Tore's solemn face and something in it opened him up. "Wickedness follows some folks, I reckon," he said. "Poor old Ignorant here's had to catch mine with me. I don't feel none too good about that, I'll tell you."

King nodded like a minister. "The Lord'll forgive, you just hold onto that." Then he smiled and said, "We'll feed your body first, how's that? Y'all hungry?"

The two both perked up and the boy, who had been holding the girl's rolled up coat under his arm, set it behind his chair and locked his hands on his knees.

King smiled even wider. "I figure I'd be hungry, too, if I was a walking all day. This rain's kept me in, though. Rained on me for three days now, and the winds have been blowing mighty hard and cold, too." He shook his head. "I was about to have supper, anyways. You boys pull them chairs to the table and we'll pass a pork stew around." He turned to the boy. "You can take that goat out to the barn now, I reckon."

When the three had positioned themselves at the table, and King had served each bowl an ample scooping of the warm, brown stew, he clasped his hands in front of him, and bent his head. The two watched him, the man bowing his head, and turning his gaze to the table.

Tore prayed, "Our dearest heavenly Father, blessed is Your name. We trust in this as surely as our salvation, o Lord. Bless our bodies with this food as you bless our soul with Christ. Keep my dear wife near you in Heaven, o Lord and keep my daughter near and forgive her her many sins, o Lord. Be with these weary travelers Lord as they leave tomorrow and bless my body for the hard work ahead. Forgive us our transgressions, o Lord. All this, I beseech in your precious name, Jesus. Amen."

"Amen," the man repeated. He looked up at the boy but could not hold the youth's confused stare. "C'mon," he said, picking up his spoon. "Eat."

In the dark of the next morning, the man showed King the dead girl's coat. King had awakened the two and set out biscuits to eat. Then he settled down by a lamp with his bible while the man had edged over to him with the bundle.

He unrolled it on a large trunk by the door. "It was our sister's," the man said. "She died not long ago, and it's all we have left of her."

King stared at it, his gray eyes hardening in his sharp, wind-burned face. But he said nothing.

"It's a fine coat, sir. Soft. Pretty. I recollect, when you was praying yesterday, that your wife and daughter was with the Lord, but I figured if you got a girl in town or somewhere's, it'd be mighty nice to give her."

King took a deep breath. His bible rested on his thigh, his finger marking a page. He set it on his reading table and took the coat in his hands, rubbing the fabric between his fingers. He held it up to the light.

"It's muddy," he said.

"Well, yes sir, it is. It's been raining these last few days." King rubbed a small blood stain on the shoulder of the coat and the man told him, "That's where Ignorant cut hisself a few days ago. It'll wash out."

King stared at it a while. "Why'd you keep it?" he asked, his voice soft and high, as if he had been crying.

The man looked down at it, his fleshy cheeks and brow bunching together. He scratched the back of his hand with his coarse beard. "I don't reckon I know really why I kept it. On account of it's still pretty, I reckon. Like she was pretty. She was a young thing, only twelve year or so. She was innocent still." He sat down. "Something in that's a might scary, to see innocence pass on." He rubbed his temples, and behind him the boy stared at the two men. "I kept it on account of that, maybe. Try to keep some of her alive. But now I got to think of the boy. I was thinking, if you had a coat that'd fit him we could trade. He's a might cold."

King looked over at the boy. The youth's face was blank and ugly, his lank mouth bursting with teeth. King stood and walked over to his own coat hanging on a hook by the door. He pulled it off and took it to the boy, handing it over as if it were something sacred.

"That's powerful kind of you, sir," the man said from behind King. "That's a Christian kindness if I ever seen one."

King turned to him and nodded. He sighed. "I best

go check my horse," he said.

He walked out to his barn in the first blue hints of dawn, and the empty serpent shed stood black in the dim light. He hurried past it. The goat was tied to the leg of his workbench in the barn, standing and staring at him, as if it had been waiting all night. King stopped at the bench and clutched the tabletop, his fingers gripping the wood as if to tear it away. His face was red, and purple bursts exploded in his vision. The only sounds in the barn were the breathing of his horse and his long fingers trembling on the table. A cry, hollow and high, rumbled in his mouth, but he bit down on it.

He breathed heavy now, his face covered with sweat. On his table were tools, and he picked up the slaughtering knife he used for pigs. He ran it over the gray sharpening stone, stopping every few moments to listen for sounds coming from the house, but he heard nothing. He tried not to think of his daughter, but he saw her smiling down at him from her horse, her pale face framed by yellow hair.

Finally, he turned to walk toward the house but, without any thought, he spun around and slashed the goat's thin, white throat. It kicked and bit him, blood staining them both, but he slashed at it again, and the goat collapsed beneath him. He thought of the two in his home. Their twisted faces, their stench of goat and mud and men. He thought of their smell in her nose, their ugly faces next to hers. He pulled himself up and ran to the house.

The man seemed to know, when the door flung open and King stood in the blood-red dawn before them, what was to happen. He almost laughed—how could this be—and sprung for the stove, hoping to get the black-iron stoker. King struck him in the shoulder with the long, hard knife, and the man screamed as his muscles split apart. Trembling, the boy crept toward the door. King caught him by the hair and flung him back over his reading table. In the same instant, the man hit King's back with the stoker. King twisted beneath him, plunging the knife into the man's abdomen. He caught the stoker in his left hand and pulled himself up, slicing open the man's abdomen. The man howled like a mountain lion and thrashed about, falling on to the floor. King, the knife lifted above his head, his face red with the man's blood, fell on him and slashed his throat open.

When he pulled himself up, he heard the boy fleeing across the wet, open field toward the woods. He ran to his room and pulled his Winchester from the wall and hurried outside. He waited until the boy was beside the single oak left in the field, and then he fired. Blood sprayed from the boy's back and he fell. When the boy began to move, King dropped the gun. He rushed to the barn and pulled some rope from the wall and ran out to the field.

The youth lay on his stomach crying, blood covering the soggy brown earth around him. King threw the rope over the lowest tree limb and tied it to the boy's neck. The boy wept, a horrible gurgling cry shaking his face, his big teeth stained with dirt. King closed his own eyes and pulled the boy into the air. A flailing foot struck his cheek, and he took a few steps back, and the rope jerked. The boy coughed. King clutched the rope, and when he realized that the jerking had stopped, he opened his eyes. The body swung above him, jaw hanging open, mouth dirty and empty.

King released the body and it dropped to the earth.

King seemed to drop with it, lying beside the dead boy in the mud as long, white branches of lightning stretched across the sky, shaking in his vision like the naked limb of a birch tree.

A shower started on his way to find her. It came through the bare trees with cold gusts of wind that pierced his clothing and frightened his horse. His face was tight, lowered to the wind and the stinging drops, and he clamped his teeth down hard.

He wanted to cry out, to yell to God. But the shower was too hard, pricking his face like needles, and he could only ride. Was the rain God's punishment? He thought of the boy lying dead in his field, the man bloody in his den. In his own home lay a man he had slain. The thought shook him worse than the rain or wind.

His hands burned with the cold, but as he clutched them tight, as if to hold on to any warmth he had left, he knew that he would always feel murder in them. He would feel it each time he took up his ax, each time he rubbed them together for warmth, each time he held his bible.

As he turned a curve in the road, he saw the box in the road. Tying the horse to a tree, he listened as rain tapped the lid. He heard the snake thumping inside. He looked around, and through the trees he saw a speck of unnatural white. He rushed through the woods, wet branches scratching his face as he went.

He dropped beside her.

Her face was clean and white. All the blood had long since drained away and her nose was crushed in, her teeth broken. But she was so white. He held her, and crying sat with her across his lap, as he had when she was young. Something in him wanted to pray, but he found that he could not. He felt that he had no more words to speak to God.

When the rain had slowed, and lighter clouds had drifted overhead, he lay her on the ground and stood up. He pulled off his shirt and wrapped it around her head. Walking through the trees, his skin gleaming in the rain, he thought to load her onto the horse and take her home. And yet, the thought of home was ugly to him now. The dead bodies there shook him, and he trembled at the thought of going back. Then he saw the box.

It lay on the muddy trail. He knelt down near it and placed his hand on the lid. The wood was ruined from the rain, the latch already beginning to rust. He could feel the snake inside, dangerous and ready. He took a deep breath and opened it.

The serpent hissed at him. Scaled and brown, its diamond-shaped head sprung out of the box. King caught it behind its jaw and clutched it tighter than he ever had before. Its tail whipped at him and coiled around his arm, and he pulled it loose with his free hand, holding it in the center. Then he turned the jaw loose. The serpent rose up in front of him, its head seeming to float in the air, its hot yellow eyes locked with his. He watched as its mouth opened, four curved teeth bared, preparing to strike.

NIGHT TERRORS

When the stranger next to me screamed in her sleep, I tumbled out of bed and smacked my face on her nightstand. Exploding red suns spun around me in the dark as she shrieked like someone was killing her. I struggled to my feet and steadied myself against the wall, trying to let my vision clear. When it did, I saw her thrashing about in blue moonlight and clawing at the sheets like she was possessed. Finally she twitched, curled into a ball, and began gently snoring.

For a moment, I just stood there naked, listening to the angry thump of my heart.

Then I realized I was bleeding. I inched my way across our clothes piled on the carpet and searched for her bathroom in the dark. When I found it, I closed the door and turned on the light.

In that sudden glare, I looked like hell. Three bright streams of blood ran down my face from a gash on my forehead. Blood dotted my chest and arms and dripped on her sink and floor. My hands still shook with adrenaline as I tried to wash up, but I finally got the job done. When everything was clean, and I was calmed down, I turned off the light.

As quietly as I could, I dressed in the dark. Normally,

I wasn't the type to sneak out in the middle of the night, but I wasn't going to stick around with a screamer. I thought about leaving a note, but I decided against it. What was there to say? Nice to meet you? Thanks for the sex? Do you know you shriek in your sleep?

Outside, the temperature dropped fifty degrees, and I considered going back inside where it was warm. Maybe crash on her couch. But, of course, the door was locked now. The Metro had stopped running, so there was nothing to do but hike home through the cold.

I was still thinking about her. What was her name? Lynn? Yes, Lynn, after Loretta Lynn she'd told me. Her dad was a big country music fan even though they weren't from the south. I nodded. That's right. Lynn. I couldn't recall her last name. She had honey-blonde hair and calculating green eyes, eyes that were always think-ing. Nice girl. We'd had a few drinks, talked about mu-sic and movies, and then we'd come back to her place, tipsy but not too drunk. A couple of condoms later, we kissed goodnight and fell asleep. I was going to give her the usual fake number in the morning.

Walking home before the sun had even begun to rise, though, I started to feel bad for not at least leaving a note.

I shrugged and braced myself as a truck rumbled past me. I'd be lucky if I didn't get mugged. And I was freez-ing my ass off. I didn't feel too bad for her.

She played a couple of songs on the jukebox. The first was "Somebody to Love" by Queen. She came back to the bar, three stools down from me. I leaned over. "Good choice," I said. "I haven't heard this song in a while."

That last part was a lie. Every time I came in this bar

someone was playing that song.

She smiled and brushed some hair back behind her ear. She was tiny—not more than five two, but she was wearing some heels to give herself another couple of inches.

"Yeah," she said with a thoughtful nod. She leaned toward me and said, "To tell you the truth, I sang this song for American Idol."

"Seriously?"

"Yeah. Didn't work, obviously. I stepped up, sang, and they told me to beat it. I didn't even get on TV." She lifted her glass as if to toast fate. "Just another piece of cattle."

I leaned over to say, "Nice to try, though."

She nodded.

I pointed at her empty glass. "Can I buy you another?"

"Sure."

The bartender was slicing up limes. I motioned to our glasses and eased down the bar.

I told her my name.

We shook. Her hands were small and soft. "I'm Lynn," she said.

Two days later, I was standing at my kitchen counter waiting on the coffee to brew when I read in the Washington Post that she'd been murdered. Her name was Lynn Byers, and she was an assistant manager at the Apple store in Arlington. I stared at her name, and my stomach turned to ice. She had been murdered the night I was with her. I tried to sit down, but my knees collapsed beneath me. I sat on the linoleum.

There was a picture of the front door of her apartment with police tape around it. In the corner of the article there was a small picture of her: Lynn sitting on a couch, laughing and pointing to someone or something off camera. It was an older picture and another hairdo, but it was her.

She'd been strangled in her bed by an unknown assailant. The police were investigating leads.

I dropped the paper. The police were investigating leads. What did that mean? I looked at my front door. I picked up the paper again. The police were investigating leads.

Oh, Jesus. They wouldn't think…No, no. Why would they?

I got to my feet. Why would they? I took the paper to the kitchen table and tried to read the article again.

A neighbor knocked on her door after seeing Lynn's shattered back window. When no answer came, the neighbor grew suspicious. When he noticed that Lynn's car was parked out front, he called the police.

Someone had broken in and murdered her after I left. That thought sunk down to the bottom of my stomach.

I touched the crusty gash on my forehead and thought of the towel stained with my blood. I'd probably dripped blood on the bed and floor, too.

I hurried to my front door and cracked it open. Empty street, empty sidewalk. A wind kicked up, shaking the maples in front of my apartment and sweeping their scarlet leaves down the sidewalk. Across the street, a man was watching his dog piss on a tree trunk. That was it.

Back inside, I didn't know which way to go. I picked up the phone, but I didn't have an idea who I might call.

The cops? They would find me anyway. I was the last

one to see her alive—

No, the killer was. That thought made me shudder. Tears sprang to my eyes.

She had been murdered, choked to death. Lynn. Lynn Byers. I hadn't even known her last name. I'd had sex with her, had been inside her body, had felt her breathing quicken and settle. And now she was dead. That thought was too horrible. I could still taste her mouth, could still feel her skin. She had a mole next to her left nipple, and I could tell she was sensitive about it when she took off her clothes. She was embarrassed, but not too embarrassed. She mostly wanted to judge my reaction. Her eyes were always thinking.

But not anymore.

I picked up my phone and punched in 911, but I hung up.

I walked a circuit between the kitchen and the den. I made myself stop and sit down and think. But then I got up again.

I prayed for the first time in fifteen years. Please God. Please God. Don't let this happen. I didn't get any farther than that when I realized that I was more scared than upset.

That thought sickened me. She was dead. I didn't really know her and she was dead and I was too scared to feel anything except fear.

I read the paper again looking for something new.

I walked to the den and back again.

I skimmed the paper again. My lungs felt like they were going to pop. I was going to lose it.

I ran and looked out the front door. A light rain was falling now, and wet leaves spread across the sidewalk like open sores.

I slammed the door shut and ran to my bedroom. After I threw on some clothes and a heavy coat, I ran out of the house without locking the front door.

I also didn't look behind me to see who might be there.

After a few minutes of hurrying nowhere in particular, I saw the Metro. I slipped inside and dashed down the escalator to the trains. A green line train pulled up as I got to the platform, and I jumped on board. A moment later, we shot down the tunnel. For the first time that morning, my heart slowed to a steady beat. My stomached settled. There were about twenty people on the train, mostly people in suits on their way to work.

Then it hit me. I was supposed to be at work. I dug in my pocket for my cell phone, but I couldn't find it. I dug through every pocket I had three times before I accepted that I'd left it on the kitchen table. I hadn't left home without it in years.

I asked a woman across the aisle for the time. She pushed back the cuff of her coat and said, "Ten-thirty."

I was supposed to be at work at nine. That realization actually stopped me for a second. I'd never been late to work. Ever. Punctuality is like a religion with me. But now I was on a train, heading the opposite direction. How would that look to the cops? I hadn't even called in to tell work I'd been late. As the train rumbled out of the tunnel, my bowels roiled like a cauldron.

I tried to calm myself. First thing: I had to go to the cops. I had to go to them and tell them what happened. I met her, we had sex, and I left. That's it. When I left, she was alive. The truth, that's all I could tell them.

We found your blood, they would say.

I fell out of bed, I'd say. She had a screaming fit in the middle of the night, and I fell out of bed and bumped my head.

And someone broke in after you left? Just happened to break in and kill Lynn Byers in the same bed? That's what you're trying to tell us?

They wouldn't believe me, but I didn't have anything else to tell them. They would find me. They would go to the bar, talk to the bartender, find out who she was talking to, check the debit card receipts. They could be at my house right now, but they'd see I wasn't there. They'd find out that I failed to show up for work today.

Next stop, I thought. At the next stop, you get off this train and get on one to take you to the cops. Get this thing settled.

I bought her another Stella and had one myself. The bartender went back to his limes.

"I've tried out for all kinds of things," she said. "TV shows, reality shows, plays, talent searches. Never got anywhere." She shrugged. "No talent."

"Well, I don't know anything about that stuff," I said "but isn't rejection a part of the game?"

"Sure, and that's what I told myself. But you have to face facts sooner or later, right? You tell yourself, everyone who ever hit it big got the door slammed in her face at some point. Then you think, well, so did all the people who never made it."

"I guess that's true."

"Yet everyone is always telling you to follow your dreams."

"I guess."

"Thing is, most dreams never become reality. So okay, Kelly Clarkson had the dream of being a world famous pop star, and now she's a world famous pop star, but the other ten million people who tried out for American Idol had exactly the same dream, and for them it was all just bullshit."

I didn't know what to say to that. She was right, but I didn't want to let her wallow in it. If she got drunk and depressed, I'd be going home alone.

"Well," I said, "most people can't sing well enough to be famous. No shame in that. You're probably good at other things."

She ignored me. "Think about the night sky. Seems full of stars, but most of the sky is just a big empty nothing. In fact, that's what makes a star shine so bright, all the nothing around it. There's only a few stars. Most of us are the nothing."

I glanced up at the bartender. He didn't look at me, but I could tell he was listening. I bet he heard a lot of sob stories.

I looked back at Lynn, and now she was staring at me. She laughed.

"The hell with it," she said. "You want to get out of here?"

When the train stopped at Fort Totten, I slid off and sat down on an empty bench. It was good to sit down and breathe in some fresh air. Rain tapped against the uncovered portion of the platform, and I sat there watching it, waiting for the next train.

A lot of people had exited the train with me and most

of them walked to the escalators.

It seemed like one guy didn't, though. People milled around on the platform—kids in Catholic school uniforms, men and women in business attire carrying satchels and briefcases, a guy in military fatigues—but something told me that one of the people who got off the train with me hadn't moved very far.

While I glanced around like I was looking at the trees and apartment buildings in the distance, I scanned the people on the platform. In a glance, though, there's nothing special about anyone.

After a minute, a train barreled up, opened its doors and released some passengers, and then all of us who were waiting got on. I glanced around to check out faces.

You're being paranoid, I thought. No one is following you.

No one unusual. No one familiar. Just people. An old man took out a hearing aid and messed with it. Two girls—one white, one black—held hands and shared the headphones on an iPod. Some people read the paper. Some people stared out the window. No one looked at me.

No one in our car.

But when I glanced at the back door, I saw that someone was watching me from the next car. He looked away when I saw him, but I'd seen his face for a good second or two.

The bartender.

I smiled. "Sure," I said. "Let's get out of here."

I waved the bartender over. He was short and blocky, with a smooth, bland face and prematurely gray hair.

I motioned at our glasses. "I need to settle up for both of us," I told him.

Lynn laughed. "Aw, you don't have to do that," she said, nudging me.

My dick got hard.

"Easier this way," I said, nudging her back. "You can get the bill next time."

She said, "I'll tell you what—you know the liquor store down the street?"

"Sure."

"Well, I live next door."

"Really? Wait a second! The little green place with the big bathtub out front?"

She laughed. "Yep, the big bathtub full of flowers. Don't ask. It was there when I moved in."

"It's cute," I said. "I always wondered about the bathtub house."

She smiled and put her hand on my forearm. "Wanna see it up close? I can buy us a bottle on the way there."

"Sounds good," I said.

The bartender handed me the bill. He didn't say a word. As I dug out my wallet, he just looked at Lynn.

My thoughts bickered while I tried to figure out what the hell do to.

It couldn't be a coincidence. Couldn't be.

I glanced at the window again, but he'd moved away.

How long had he been following me?

Why?

The train slowed and came to a stop at New York Avenue and people got off. Others got on. I stayed where I was and watched the platform, but I didn't see him.

We pulled away from the station, and I switched seats to get a look at the next car from another vantage point.

He was there all right, wearing a nondescript brown coat and blue shirt. He stood by the door trying to blend in. His face was as smooth as a child's, but his hair was nearly completely gray. When he caught me looking at him, he flinched and moved to another seat. We stared at each other through the cars for a moment, but I was the only one who was frightened.

I opened the doors between cars walked in and sat down next to him. People glanced at us and then glanced away.

I said, "Why are you following me?"

"Here's what's gonna happen," he said under his breath. "Next stop, we're getting off. Just so we can talk."

I took a deep breath and something odd happened. I thought of Lynn. I thought of the way she'd screamed in her sleep. I would never know what her nightmares were about, and I would never want to know how horrible the waking nightmare had been when this man crept into her room and murdered her, but in that moment I felt an anger rising that dissipated the fear.

My hands steadied. They went dry. My entire body seemed to cool. I turned to him.

"Why her?" I asked.

He glanced around at the other people on the car. No one was paying us any attention.

"Why?" I said. "Why Lynn?"

The train began to slow, and he turned to me and jerked his head at the sliding doors. "Get up. Let's go talk about this somewhere."

"There was no reason, was there? You just wanted to

hurt somebody. You saw her, and you wanted to hurt somebody, so you decided it would be her."

"I told you to get up."

"What'd you do, follow me home that night and then go back and kill her? If you were smart you'd just let the cops pin this on me, but you didn't think of that, did you? You're too much of a sick fucking psycho. You just wanted to hurt someone."

The train lurched to a stop.

He pulled a gun from under his coat long enough to show it to me then put it in his pocket. "Get up now," he whispered "or I'll start shooting. I'll kill everybody on this train, starting with you."

I got up and he followed me to the doors. A crowd waited impatiently on the platform, and we had to push our way through them. He kept one hand on my back and one on his gun, but I spun around suddenly and grabbed his wrist and shoved it deeper into his pocket. I rammed my knee into his balls. "Gun!" I yelled. "He's got a gun!"

The place erupted. Everyone seemed to move at once. People around us heaved through the train doors trying to scramble inside as the people inside the train tried to rush out. Then the gun blasted a hole in his pocket and everything barreled into a roar that echoed down the darkened tunnel. As people stampeded us, I kept my hand on his wrist. Some guy grabbed him in a choke hold and then other people—men and women—piled on him. It was chilling to see a horde descend so quickly on one person. The sheer power of the group surged like an undercurrent dragging a hapless swimmer down. Blood pounded through my veins. I could feel the blood pounding in the crowd around me. I thought we might trample him to death.

Soon enough, though, the cops pushed their way through. Hands tightened around my arms and shoulders. Someone pulled me off of him.

Bloodied and nearly crushed, he was taken away on a stretcher once the EMT guys showed up. I was hauled in for questions, but when they found his gun, along with my address scribbled down on the back of my debit card bill, they pieced it all together. After a few hours, they took my statement and let me go home.

That night, I rode home on the Metro in a daze. People bustled around me, but nothing seemed quite solid or connected. When I got off the train, I staggered home like a drunk man.

Even though I was exhausted, it took a while for me to fall asleep. At three the next morning when I finally drifted off, I dreamed that Lynn was lying in bed next to me. I knew she would scream, that whatever had scared her would come back, and I wanted to tell her she'd be okay. I wanted to say that this time I wouldn't run away.

But I couldn't. I had no mouth, just a deep, thick scar where a gash had sealed shut. All I could do was lie next to her in the darkness. Her breathing grew erratic. I couldn't breathe at all. When she screamed, I jerked awake.

DINNER WITH FRIENDS

Maggie liked the Bannermans, but I wasn't too fond of them. Nathan Bannerman was a wrestling coach at his son's junior high school. He was a five-foot-two tower of insecurity, and when I stood next to him I always got the faint impression he was trying to size me up for a leg sweep and a choke hold. When I was with him, we talked about sports and traffic, and I amused myself by thinking up different ways to kill him with whatever happened to be nearby. Nancy Bannerman was a profoundly overweight woman who kept putting on pounds in new areas of her body. Her chin had disappeared into her neck, which in turn had disappeared into the fleshy sphere of her torso. Because she relied so much on the charity and tact of other people, she was effusively nice. But I felt the Bannermans were both secretly shallow and boring. If they were thin, attractive, and successful, I think they would have been unbearable. Still, Maggie and Nancy were cousins, so a few times a year I had to endure a dinner with them.

We were sitting at a seafood restaurant one night listening to Nathan Bannerman rattle on about some unruly eighth grader, and I let my mind wander back over the day. That afternoon, I had killed a man named Art

Thomas in a spacious loft apartment in lower Manhattan, within walking distance to the man's job in the financial district. I don't know what he did for a living, but he must have been good at it to afford such a swank place that close to all the money in the world.

Nathan Bannerman leaned over to me, "I told that little bastard, 'I'm a grown man. You're an eighth grader. Got me, buster?'" Bannerman stared at me, eager to see if I was impressed.

"Whoa," I said. "What'd he say?"

I knew that would elicit a five-minute reply, so while Bannerman yammered on, I thought about Art Thomas. He had been a pudgy gray haired man with wire rim glasses and when I saw him today, he was wearing a thousand-dollar pair of pants.

He came up his stairs, unlocked his door, and was sorting his mail at the kitchen counter when I walked out of his bedroom and shot him in the back of the head. He hit the counter and slumped to the floor, and I shot him twice more in the back of the head. By that point, there wasn't much left to shoot.

The piece had come from Thomas's bedroom closet. I left it at the scene, and shoved my latex gloves into a large McDonald's cup. I carried the cup downstairs and over to Broad Street where I dumped it in the trash before I caught the subway uptown.

Maggie and Nancy laughed at something Bannerman had said. I chuckled and slapped him on the shoulder.

The waiter came over and suggested dessert, and before I could say anything, my wife asked to see the menu.

"Oh, I shouldn't," Nancy said.

"Oh, c'mon. We'll spilt it," Maggie suggested. If history were any kind of teacher, though, she'd have to race

Nancy for the last bite.

Bannerman asked me how the business was going.

"Pretty well," I said.

"Maggie said you went up to Connecticut today."

"Yeah. Had a meeting with a guy."

"Yeah, I had some meetings today, too."

Bannerman was incapable of asking two questions in a row. It was simply too much time spent away from the subject of his own utterly banal existence. He seemed to feel he was losing ground if the discussion wasn't about his shitty job, his dreary personal life, or his uninformed, backwater political views.

He finished a beer—his fourth—and I thought about smashing the glass over his nose and slitting his throat with a shard of the breakage.

Bannerman sighed. "Yeah, I don't know. Those people up there at the school, they're a good bunch. They try to be, anyway. But they haven't been the same since old Dale Hudson died."

That stopped me.

"Dale Hudson died?"

"Yeah. Last year."

"Last year," Nancy affirmed.

Maggie looked at me. "Who's Dale Hudson?"

"He was the principal," I told her.

I'd attended Edward Q. Brooks High School the year my father died. My mother had married a man from our church within a few months of my father's death, and we had moved to another town to live with him and his two sons. The boys, both of them a little older than me, were never very nice to me, but they mostly left me alone. When I started attending school with them in the fall, they kept their distance from me in the halls and the cafeteria. I suppose it was lonely, though it could have been worse.

Dale Hudson was a tall, gray-haired man with a paunch and a seemingly endless supply of short-sleeved white shirts. The kids mostly either mocked him or hated him, though I don't recall him being particularly absurd or cruel. He was just a bored functionary, a man going about his job. I hadn't given him any thought in twenty years.

The waiter brought the dessert menu and the girls chose a cheesecake. Bannerman ordered a crème brûlée, pronouncing it "cream brew-lee," and asked for another beer to tide him over until it got there. I had coffee.

"Dale Hudson died," I said.

Maggie watched my face.

"You seem fascinated by that," she said.

I smiled. "I just...I don't know, I hadn't thought about him in a long time. It's odd to hear that he died."

"He was an old man," Bannerman said. "I hope I'm going strong like him in the end."

I said, "I hadn't thought of him as being old. I guess I thought he was still fifty-whatever years old, still schlepping the halls of Edward Q. Brooks, telling kids to get to class. I hadn't thought about his life still, you know, still going on when I wasn't there."

Nancy's bulk shifted beneath her tent-like green dress, and she said, "I think that's as many words as I've ever heard you speak at one time."

The three of them laughed, and I smiled.

Bannerman said, "I think that's about as many words as I've ever heard him speak at one time, too"—which was his way of stealing his wife's line. He did that all the time. If you said something interesting or funny, Bannerman would repeat it like he'd just thought of it himself. Insufferable little shit.

Still, as the dessert arrived and the conversation moved back to what it had been all night—Nancy's commentary on the food and Bannerman's commentary on himself—I stared at the little man and wondered what he did with his days.

It's not too much to say that I lack some seemingly essential component of human compassion. I'm not sure why that is. I've thought about it over the years. I have two theories.

One, I'm an anomaly, a freak of nature, an exception to the rule. If there's a god—which seems unlikely—then he or she or it made me what I am. Nature just made a mistake, like a baby born without arms. My lack of compassion is a genetic defect.

My second theory is that I'm nothing particularly special. Wars have been fought every year for as long as we've recorded history, and most of the people who killed each other in these wars had no good reason to do it. Sadists kill because they get off on human suffering. Mothers sometimes snap and drown their children in the bathtub. Sometimes men lose their jobs and strangle their ex-wives. Gangbangers shoot each other because they're too stupid to do anything else. And on and on.

But sometimes people decide to kill someone else just to make life a little easier on themselves—to free up some cash, or to enact a revenge they themselves are not capable of following through on. Then they talk to someone who talks to someone who talks to me. And I take care of it.

My only virtue—and it's not much of a virtue I'll grant—is that I'm as cold as Pluto. I'm not a sadist or a psycho. I'm not out to rule the world or get my kicks from watching people die. I'm coldly indifferent, yes, but I don't think I'm at all unique in this indifference. It's just that most people are acceptably indifferent to the pain and suffering of other people. It's okay not to care about people dying in other countries, or even down the street, because you don't know them. An utter and complete lack of compassion is acceptable in a macro sense. I just feel that in a micro sense.

Sure, I'll admit I like the surge of adrenaline I get when I'm on the job. Before I started in business, I did a variety of extreme things—skydiving, rock climbing— just to get the rush. But now I get the rush from the job.

Sitting in Art Thomas's bedroom that afternoon, I'd felt my pulse quicken as I heard the elevator down the hall. I didn't know anything about the man other than his taste in home décor was impeccable. I didn't know why someone wanted him dead. Maybe he molested their kid. Maybe his wife was a selfish asshole who wanted his will to kick in to effect sooner rather than later. I don't know. But my heart was pounding when he turned the key in the door and came inside. When he walked across his living room, his shoes squeaking against his hardwood floors. When his head exploded, he hit the counter and died at my feet. My blood was pumping as I left his building and walked down the street, the sun on my face, people passing by, not paying a bit of attention to the thoroughly ordinary man walking by with a big cup from MacDonald's. I could have been anybody. Art Thomas. Dale Hudson. Even Nathan Bannerman.

I didn't have anything against Art Thomas. I was there was an instrument of someone else's longing. If not me, it would have been some other instrument. If Bannerman had thought of it first, and if he had the actual physical courage necessary to do it, no morality would have stopped him from doing what I did.

So why shouldn't it be me?

CASUAL ENCOUNTER

The Craigslist thing started innocently. At that time, I was working as a tech writer for a company that designed educational software, and I needed something to do in my spare time. Like every other bored, stumbling-toward-middle-age married white guy, I decided I would learn to play the guitar. I went on Craigslist to find a cheap one, but then I drifted over to the Men Seeking Women section. Just to see what it was like. I rooted around in there for a few days, and then I took the leap into the section for Casual Encounters.

It was a crazy place to be (and it felt like being in a place rather than just sitting on the couch looking at a screen). It was, simply put, a place where people were hunting for sex. Even if you figured that ninety-nine percent of the posts were bullshit, that still left one percent of an endless ocean of indecency. And it was so raw. People weren't coy. They wanted to fuck in the park at night. They wanted to cheat on their spouses. Women wanted to fuck in the broom closet at work, in public places during business hours, in restrooms at random gas stations. Some didn't care what you looked like. Some wanted fat guys.

I figured I'd post an ad on a lark. What the hell. It was

all in fun. I'd never actually do…it. And I really, seriously thought I never would. How could I? Meet a stranger for sex? I'd only had sex with two people in my life. I'd post the ad just to get off on the thrill of doing it.

And it worked. Just posting the damn thing sent a cocaine jolt through my body:

Guy in his twenties looking for a high school or college girl for sexy fun times. Let's get crazy.

I felt like an idiot writing it. Sounds idiotic. Hell, it is idiotic. But that's how people talk on there. That kind of asinine language is shorthand for I'm dead serious about this. I'm not trying to be charming. Contact me if you want to get fucked.

A few days passed. Nothing happened. I actually got really depressed about that for a day. I'd check in every five minutes and…nothing. I couldn't even get an anonymous stranger to flirt with me on the internet. What kind of loser fails at that?

And I didn't need the rejection right then. My marriage was barely functioning since I'd found out that my wife was having an affair. She was a shift manager at Barnes & Noble, and the dude she'd fucked was a waiter at a Mexican restaurant in the same strip mall. They went to a motel and put it on our credit card. Since she usually paid that bill, she thought I'd never see it. The motel made a mistake, though, and charged her three times for the same visit. Computer error. That same afternoon I was going through the drive-thru at KFC without any cash and had to use my card. When it was declined, I called VISA and some bored call center operator in Bangladesh told me, in so many words, that my wife was banging someone on her lunch breaks.

We'd gotten through that—by which I mean the guy

dumped her and she stayed with me—and I tried not to hold it against her. I mean, if I could have banged a waitress at a motel, I'm sure I would have. I'd stayed faithful because I didn't have any other choice.

But then a girl named Traci wrote me back on Craigslist and asked what I was up to.

My stomach dropped. I wrote back and said Nothing. What about you?

And that's how it began. It went on for days. She was interested. She'd had sex like this before, and she loved it. Nothing serious. Just some fun. She asked how big my dick was. She said she could meet me. Then she said she was fifteen.

When I read those words some distant door slammed shut. I was alone, but my face started burning like the whole world was watching me. I wasn't sure how I got there. To be honest and up front with her, I told Traci I was thirty-two. I asked if that was cool. She said it was. The last guy was forty, she said. She liked older guys.

I debated it. It was crazy. But, she'd had experience. Maybe even more than me. Plus, all the kids are doing it these days, right?

We decided to meet the next day. My wife would be at work. Perfect. I'd pick Traci up, and we'd find a place. After I Google-mapped the nearest park that night, I could barely sleep. At midnight, I had diarrhea. For the rest of the night, I just stared at shadows on the ceiling and listened to my wife's acid reflux. The next morning, I got up, locked the bathroom door and jerked off. I thought that would diminish the desire to go meet Traci, but it didn't.

After my wife left for work, I took a shower. I clipped my nosehairs and my fingernails. I put on clean clothes and splashed on some cologne that was a seven-year-old Christmas present from my mother-in-law. Then I drove over to the park. I rode in silence. I've never been as scared of anything in my life as I was that first time.

I rode around the park. Every girl seemed to be Traci. She was a brunette with brown eyes. I saw a half-dozen girls who fit the description, but she said she'd be wearing a green skirt and a red tank-top. No Traci. I drove around for an hour. No Traci. I got out. Walked around. I got back in my car and went home.

Her message was waiting for me. She'd chickened out.

I told her I thought she wanted this.

You've done this before, right?

yes

You don't have to do it. You know that.

i know but i want to. Its just im nervous.

But you did it before.

i was nervous then to

After a while, we agreed to meet. This time, she'd meet me at the motel.

The next day I wasn't as scared. You can't build up the same rush again. I was anxious, but my nerves had been shot the day before. I didn't jerk off this time, either.

As I was leaving, my wife was sitting at the kitchen table, staring at her laptop. I told her I was going to go to the mall and see if GameStop had the new whatever.

She didn't look up from the screen. "I might call you later to tell you to pick up some stuff at the grocery store," she said. She double clicked on something. "Make sure you leave your phone on."

"Why would I have it off?"

"What?"

"Why would I turn my phone off?"

She frowned at the screen and clicked on something. "Just make sure you leave it on," she said.

I said okay and left.

I zipped through the city streets. I sped the whole way. I caught every yellow light. I got there at noon. I'd check in, text her, and Traci would show up ten minutes later.

At the front, an elderly Asian man in a Superman t-shirt was working the counter. He took my card. Since my wife's affair, I'd been in charge of the credit cards. Karma's a bitch.

The old man took down my information. He gave me a key attached to a piece of plastic with a faded number twenty-seven on it.

I walked outside, around to room twenty-seven and unlocked the door. There was the bed. I texted Traci: Room twenty-seven. Come and get me.

The cop who arrested me was an attractive black woman with a square jaw and bemused eyes. Her name was Trenita Ohakim. I remember it from the trial. O-ha-kim. She handcuffed me while two other cops—both men—looked on, smirking. They didn't take their job seriously. Or maybe they just thought I was the butt of a joke.

I wanted to cry, but I couldn't. I couldn't even feel enough at that moment to cry. I said, "May I go to the bathroom?"

"You'll have to wait," Officer Ohakim said.

"I can't," I said. "Really. I think I'll piss on the seat of your car."

She uncuffed me and one of the other cops led me to the bathroom and stared at me while I unzipped my pants and took out my pathetic dick. We stood there in silence.

"Want me to turn on some water?" he asked.

"Sure."

Behind me, water splashed against the sink.

They put me in the back of Officer Ohakim's car. The seat was hot and smelled like old plastic.

As she drove, I said, "I wasn't looking for underage girls."

She didn't say anything for a while. I wasn't sure she heard me.

When we stopped at a light, she leaned to her right as if she was looking at something in the seat beside her. She said, "You specified high school girls."

The light turned green.

I looked down at my clothes. Jeans fresh out of the laundry. A red button-up shirt. I had picked them out because I thought Traci would find me attractive in them.

My face burned.

"Were you the one writing the posts?" I asked Officer Ohakim.

"Yes."

I looked out the window. We were turning down my street.

"Wait, why are we here?" I asked her. I broke out in a sweat. "Oh Jesus. Please don't do this." Tears surged to my eyes, but I held them back. "Please, officer."

"We have to seize your computer," she said. "Is your wife still at home?"

They knew I was married. Of course they did. This was happening. There was no warning. This was happening now.

I started to cry. Not hard. Not sobbing. But there was no sucking it in.

"Yes," I sputtered.

We stopped and one of the cops in the car behind us got out and walked up to Officer Ohakim's window. He asked her, "Is his wife at home?"

"Yeah."

He left and walked up the path to the door of our apartment and knocked.

I looked away when the door opened.

After a moment, Officer Ohakim said, "She wants to see your face, sir."

I turned. My wife was standing in our apartment doorway looking around the officer. When she saw me, she put her hand to her mouth and started crying. He had to help her steady herself against the doorframe. She looked fat and pathetic and stupid. I know, because I caused her to look that way. She had been sitting at the kitchen table looking like a regular person, and then a police officer knocked on her door and told her that her husband was under arrest for soliciting sex from a minor. I'd only been gone from the house about thirty-five minutes.

He followed her inside. A few minutes later, he came back outside carrying my laptop. My wife came to the door and looked at me. She put her hand to her mouth just as she had before, just as if it was happening all over again.

* * *

129

I was convicted, but I got released early after thirteen months. First time offender. Crowded jails. My lawyer argued that I was an idiot but not a monster and added that I'd already lost my wife and my job when the story hit the papers. The judge gave me an ass-chewing and told me to get out of his face and make damn sure I never came back. I'm on parole for five years, and I have to register as a sex offender everywhere I live for basically the rest of my life.

Because I can't reside within six hundred feet of anywhere kids play or go to school, I live out on the edge of the city. I sleep in a lean-to under an underpass and my only neighbors are two weepy child-molesters and an old man who did sixty years in prison for a string of rapes in the 1950s.

Now that I have no friends, I spend my days talking to myself in my lean-to, obsessing over everything that fell apart. I don't know how accurate my memory is anymore, though. I've thought about it so much, it's like a picture that's faded and crumbling at the edges.

When I can work, I do day labor. Lately, I've been doing this job, sitting in this booth at this car lot. It's a sweltering little box. The boss doesn't allow us to watch TV or read on the clock. So I sit here and sweat and talk to myself for eight hours. It's not hard work. In fact, it isn't really work. Work would at least feel like something. This is just an endless nothing. I sit here and sweat and wait for nothing.

Two days ago, near the end of my shift, I'm sitting here sweating when I see Officer Ohakim. She was with a guy. They pulled into my lot and parked and walked out past my box on their way to the restaurant next door. The guy was handsome, with amber skin and a shaved head. He wore a gray suit. Officer Ohakim wore a navy blue dress. Looked like a first date to me.

As they walked past me, the man was laughing and saying, "I am for sure Roxy never said any such thing about you."

Officer Ohakim giggled. "Well, you are for sure wrong."

The man glanced at me and nodded. I nodded back. Officer Ohakim looked at me, smiled politely, and then when my face clicked for her, she stopped smiling. She stared down at her toenails. They were painted bright blue. She and the man walked to the sidewalk, and waiting for the light to turn, far enough away that I couldn't hear, she leaned over and told him the only thing about me that anyone remembers anymore.

THE THEOLOGIANS

It wasn't bad enough that I totaled my car when I tried to drive it through my ex-girlfriend's doublewide—now I had to attend these stupid meetings. The kicker was that the judge said I was getting off easy. I wasn't going to prison for attempted murder. I wasn't going to prison at all. Aside from the thirty-two days I spent in the lockup in Little Rock, all I had to do was complete a bunch of community service and attend weekly meetings for recovering alcoholics.

That last part was the lawyer's big brainstorm. She was a tired little woman in an old skirt and tennis shoes. She spoke to me for maybe five minutes before she walked into court and convinced the judge I was a drunk.

When we walked out, I told her, "I'm not an alcoholic."

"Good," she said. "Then the meetings should be the easiest part of this whole deal."

Since I didn't have a car anymore, getting to meetings every week was a real pain. After picking up garbage in an orange vest on the side of the highway all day, I didn't feel like hiking over to the community center for the AA meetings. Instead, I ended up going to something called Free At Last just down the road from my apart-

133

ment. I didn't think anything when I saw that meetings were held in the basement of a church, but once I got in there I realized Free At Last was a Christian drug rehabilitation program.

I didn't say shit at the first couple of meetings. I just sat there while people talked. They were a pretty sad bunch. One middle-aged woman was there because she rear-ended a school bus after an all-night bender. A young guy—younger than me—said his wife was tired of him passing out and pissing in their bed. And some other guy, twenty years sober, said he stopped drinking after he showed up drunk to a Christmas party and threw up all over someone's nativity scene. In short, a bunch of losers. They all cried about what assholes they'd been, and then they all congratulated themselves on getting Jesus to clean up the mess they'd made of their lives. I guess Jesus even forgave the guy who puked in the manger.

At the third Free At Last meeting, a woman I hadn't really noticed before came up to me after the share time was over.

"We haven't met," she said. "I'm Sadie."

We shook. "Ray."

"You haven't said anything yet, Ray."

I shrugged. Sadie was tall for a woman, taller than me and half of the other guys in the room, with big hips and some paper-bag-brown hair she pulled back in a ponytail. She didn't seem friendly exactly, just forward. I couldn't tell if she was criticizing me or trying to pick me up.

"No," I said. I pulled at the bottom of my t-shirt, making sure it covered my gut, and stuck a thumb through the belt loop of my jeans. "To tell the truth, I have to be here. Court order."

"Hm. No kidding. That's interesting."

I tried to remember something she had said at the meetings. She hadn't spoken that night. She had just sat there, like me, staring at the floor while other people talked about pissing their life away on Jim Beam and Captain Morgan.

I followed the rest of the group through the basement of the church and out the back door. It led into the parking lot. A couple of people had family or friends waiting to pick them up. The rest got in their cars.

Sadie asked, "So what'd you do to get tossed in jail?"

I stopped and stared at her. "That's personal. You know? Private?"

She nodded and looked around the parking lot. The last couple of people were leaving. That left only one car in the lot, a late-90s Nissan Altima with a chipped paint job and no passenger side mirror. Her car, I figured.

"You walking?" she asked.

"Yeah."

"Want a ride?"

I almost laughed at that. This chick either wanted to save me or fuck me. "I don't know you," I said. "We just met."

"Yeah," she said, digging the keys out of the pocket of her jeans. "But I have something I want to talk to you about. So, do you want to walk home or do you want a ride?"

It turned out that she didn't want to sleep with me or talk about my everlasting soul.

She pulled up in front of my apartment building and rolled down her window and lit a Camel Blue. She offered me one, but I shook my head.

"It's a pretty simple job," she said. "We scope out the obituaries. When someone dies who looks like they might have something worth stealing, we wait until the funeral. Then we break in and rob the place. Some old lady is at the cemetery burying her husband, and we're at her house carrying off her good china."

"I'm not a thief," I said. "I've never done anything like that."

"What do you do for a living?"

"I work at KFC."

"How old are you?"

"Thirty-two."

"Thirty-two years old and you're frying chicken at KFC. How's that working out for you?"

"Mostly I'm on the register."

"Oh, well, heck. Get out of the way, world, we got a success story coming through."

"Fuck you, bitch," I said. "You don't know me."

She just nodded and pulled at her cigarette. "Hey, sweetie, you ain't gotta get mean. I'm not talking bad about you. I got a crap job, too. Night shift at the Supercenter, grocery side. I stock shelves. You bought any beans at Walmart in the last couple years, chances are I put them there. But now I'm thinking about making some money on the side. I'm thirty-five years old and I got two kids. One's got autism. You got any idea what it costs to have a nine year old with autism?"

"No."

"A lot. Freaking doctors and tests and all kinds of bullcrap. And the worst part is, I know my son's not ever going to get half of what he needs. Autism is a rich person's condition. Ain't easy to manage working the night shift at Walmart."

"Okay," I said.

"You got a wife, girlfriend, anything like that?"

"Not anymore."

"You a drunk?"

"No."

"Why do you have to attend the meetings?"

"Drove through a girl's bedroom two days after we broke up. I thought she was in bed with a friend of mine. Turns out, they were having dinner at Red Lobster."

"I figured it was something like that," she said.

"Why are you asking me to go along on this with you? Why not ask a friend?"

She stared at the end of her cigarette. "I ain't got no friends. None that I could bring in on a situation like this, anyway. When I saw you across the room, the way you sat there listening to everything with that court-mandated look on your face, I could tell you'd be up for a good deal like this." She thought about that as her cigarette burned out at the filter. She flicked it into the parking lot. "So tell me, was I wrong?"

Her voice crackled over the phone. "You read the paper today?"

"I didn't say you could call me here."

I was standing in the doorway of the manager's office talking on his desk phone. He was out front, and although he was a pretty good guy, I didn't want to press my luck. When he'd come out to the registers to tell me I had a call, he'd looked a little irritated.

"I'll make it quick," she said. "Did you see the obits?"

"Yes," I said. I'd been getting the paper just to read

the obituaries every day since we'd talked. "I didn't see anything."

"Mildred Redding. Read it again. You coming to the meeting tonight?"

"Sure."

"We'll talk then."

Mildred Redding was eighty-four years old when she died. She'd left behind a husband named Tom, two kids, five grandkids, and one great-grandkid. She'd been a member of the First Church of Christ and of several social organizations. The obituary reported that she was now in heaven with her Blessed Savior. Her funeral was on Friday.

"I started drinking when I was a teenager," Sadie shared.

People around the circle nodded.

"It was just something the kids in my town did. It wasn't seen as anything that bad. We all went down the river and drank after football games. Mostly beer. I drank a lot. I guess I was nervous. I drank a lot so I wouldn't be so nervous. It worked. Loosened me up. And, added bonus, it seemed to make the boys like me more. I was never pretty. I was always a little too big, a little too plain. But get me drunk enough and some of them football players who usually made fun of me in between classes, all the sudden they'd want to hang around and get real friendly. I guess that made me the town slut. That's what people said anyway. Never said that about the boys, though. They weren't bad for having sex with me, but I was bad for having sex with them.

They were just being boys. Me, I was…bad. I was broken. I was wrong. At the time, I didn't think that was hypocritical, I just figured it was true.

"That went on into my twenties. I got pregnant. Had a kid. Got pregnant again. Had an abortion. No rhyme or reason to why I kept one and got rid of the other. It wasn't because of the men involved. They were all the same. I got pregnant a third time, and I kept the child. After that, I gave up alcohol. Once I gave up alcohol, I didn't have to give up the men. They just stopped coming around.

"No offense to any of the men here. I'm sure you guys are doing your best. But, ladies, the only man I ever met that I could count on was Jesus Christ. He was a virgin. You ever think about that? Catholics make a big deal out of Mary being a virgin, but I think people should think more about Jesus being a virgin. Bible never says he wrestled with sex. He had his mind on higher things. That's why I love Jesus. That's why I count on him. I don't have to reach for a beer, anymore. I don't have to reach out for some man. Cause I'm holding onto Jesus."

As we were pulling out of the church parking lot after the meeting she asked me, "You read Mildred Redding's obit?"

"Yes."

"Well?"

"Why her?"

"I smell money there. Old lady. Married, kids, grandkids. The house is over in Hillside, nice neighborhood. I bet you the house is two stories. She belonged to the Toastmistresses, for crying out loud."

"I don't know what that is."

"It ain't anything that poor people would waste their time on, I can tell you that. She'll have jewelry and china. We can hock stuff like that. I know a guy."

"Won't the cops check the pawn shops?"

"This ain't a pawn shop. Plus, my guy's in Memphis. Cops here won't check there."

"What if her kids divvy up the jewelry before the funeral?"

"They won't. No one does that. You wait till the old lady is laid to rest, then you start fighting over who gets what."

"Okay. So what do you want to do?"

"I say we drive over there right now and scope it out. Then we go in on Friday. Funeral's at noon. You work Friday?"

"From three to eleven."

"More than enough time."

"Okay," I said. "But how do we go about it?"

She drove toward Hillside.

"Just like I said."

"Neighbors won't notice?"

"It's noon on a Friday. People will be at work. Anyone on the street who cares about the Reddings are probably going to be at the funeral."

That made sense. "You know what," I said. "We should dress up. Like in funeral clothes. We show up with pots, like we're bringing over a pot roast or something. That way if anyone does see us, they'll think we're just there to set up for dinner or something."

"That's good," she said. "I like that."

"Shit," I said.

"What?"

"What if someone is really there to do that? You know? If the family comes back to the house after the funeral to have lunch or a pot luck or whatever..."

"We'll be gone by then."

"But I mean, what if someone stays at the house to set up instead of going to the funeral?"

"That won't happen."

"How do you know?"

"It won't. People go to the funeral, and they pay their respects. No one skips the funeral to go to the house to set up. We'll be in and out as quick as we can. On the off chance that someone is there early, we'll roll with it. Just say we knew her from the freaking Toastmistresses."

The house was perfect. Even I had to admit it—and I was clearly the worrier of our little operation. It was two stories with tall hedges around the sides of the house. It had a lot of yard, which meant that the nearest house was too far away to give anyone much a view of what we were doing.

We drove past the place a couple of times that night. The lights were on, and a couple of cars filled in the driveway.

"Probably the kids come to visit the old man," she said. "They'll all be at the funeral on Friday."

I nodded at that, but realizing it was true made me feel bad.

As Sadie left Hillside and headed to my apartment, I said, "Kind of a shitty thing to do, isn't it? Stealing from some old man who just lost his wife."

She didn't respond to that right away. She just stared at her headlights, one slightly cocked inward, as they clawed at the road in front of us.

"It's just stuff," she said finally. "No one needs stuff. What's he going to do with his wife's old junk? What are his kids going to do with it?"

"You know, hand it down to the grandkids."

"No one needs stuff," she said again. "I need money. So do you. None of them needs that old stuff as much as we need the money."

I wore the best dark shirt I had, and I matched it with my pair of gray slacks. I looked like I was on my way to church. When Sadie came to pick me up, she was wearing a blue top and a black skirt.

"We look pretty respectable," she said.

"Did you bring some pots?"

She jerked her head toward the backseat. "Brought a couple."

We didn't say much as we drove over to the Redding residence. I kept taking deep breaths. Sadie put a cigarette in her mouth, but she never lit it. When we got to Hillside and she turned down the street to the house, she removed the unlit cigarette from her mouth and mashed it out in the ashtray.

It was a sunny Friday afternoon, but no one on the street looked to be home. No cars in driveways. No kids playing outside, no old ladies sitting by the windows. The Redding driveway was empty, so Sadie pulled in and drove right up to the house. She reached in the backseat and handed me an empty blue crock-pot.

"Okay," she said.

We got out. Sadie carried a flowered casserole dish. The day was hot, and I was already sweating.

Sadie walked up to the front door and knocked. We waited. She knocked again. We waited. She tried the door but it was locked. She pulled out a cell phone and held it to her ear, which was a nice touch. She even went through with a fake conversation.

I thought that was a bit much. No one seemed to be watching us, and no one could hear her. But I guess it made her feel better to think that she was covering her bases. I guess it made me feel better, too.

"Hey, we're here at Mildred's house. No one seems to be home, and we want to start getting ready for everybody. What should we do? Okay. Okay."

She hung up.

"I'll try around back," she said.

Carrying her dish, she disappeared into the bushes at the side of the house.

For a moment, I was all alone. I stood there with my crock-pot. I tried not to look around. I tried to look bored.

After a while of standing there sweating, I heard footsteps inside. I caught my breath as the door opened, but it was Sadie.

I followed her inside and locked the door.

"The back door was unlocked," she said.

The house had that old person smell. Nothing looked particularly valuable, though. Cheap porcelain knick-knacks of butterflies and angels. A commemorative plate with Ronald Reagan on it. A 9/11 commemorative plate with some firemen on it.

While I looked around, Sadie disappeared into the back.

I walked down the carpeted hallway and found her in the master bedroom. She was going through the old woman's jewelry case.

"Check upstairs," she said.

I nodded. For some reason, I was afraid to speak, as if someone might hear me.

Upstairs, I found a guest room with more butterfly and angel junk. Down the hall, I found an office. A desk scattered with papers, a poster of the Constitution on the wall. Some books. I pulled open the desk drawers. In the bottom drawer, I found a tin box with a lock. It was a cheap little lock that came with a key. I was about to try to pry the box open with a pair of scissors on the desk when it occurred to me to open the top drawer. Sure enough, there among the paper clips was the key.

I opened the box. Some legal looking papers. A checkbook for Mr. and Mrs. Tom Redding. An envelope. In the envelope, four hundred and forty dollars in twenties and fifties.

I closed the box, wiped it down, put it back in the drawer, returned the key, and went downstairs.

I carried the money envelope down in my hand, and Sadie smiled when she saw it. At that moment, I wished I'd stuck it in my pants and told her I'd come up short.

She asked, "How much?"

"Four forty," I whispered.

"Why are you whispering?"

I shrugged.

She held up her casserole dish. "I got some good stuff, too. We done?"

I nodded and dropped the envelope in the dish.

"Then let's get out of here," she said. "Don't forget my crock-pot."

* * *

I didn't breathe again until we were miles away and Sadie put the windows down.

Looking through the stuff in her pot, I could see why she was excited about the haul. A diamond ring, two ruby rings, some pearls. Several gold necklaces and bracelets. As near I could tell, it was all real.

"This is a great haul," I said, sticking the pot in the backseat. "How much you think we'll get?"

She got on the interstate heading for Memphis. We were driving through rice country now. On either side of the road, the only thing to look at were miles and miles of little green rice plants soaking up the sun.

"Don't know," she said. "We'll see what the guy says. Good lord willing, it'll be enough for me to get some stuff paid off."

I felt damn good. My heart had calmed down, and I leaned back and closed my eyes and just felt the warm wind slapping at my arm. "This was a fucking great idea, Sadie."

"I know. It worked out real nice."

"We gonna do this again?"

"You bet your butt."

I smiled.

"Everything works out," she said with a satisfied sigh, "for the good of them that love the lord."

"What?"

"Romans 8:28."

"You quoting the Bible?"

"Yeah."

I laughed. "I guess it's good to memorize some of that shit to keep up appearances."

She didn't say anything. When I opened my eyes, she was frowning. Her whole forehead seemed scrunched down damn near to her eyebrows. "What are you talking about?" she asked.

"To keep up appearances. To make people think you're a Christian and stuff."

"I can't believe you'd say that to me."

"What?"

"I am a Christian."

"Yeah but…"

"But what?"

"You don't really believe…all that stuff…" I stopped talking then because I knew I'd stepped in some shit.

"Wait," she said. "Are you telling me you don't believe in god?"

"Me? Not…really."

"Stop it," she said, as if I'd just said the most absurd thing she'd ever heard.

"What? I don't."

"What kind of idiot doesn't believe in god? How'd we all get here if there's no god?"

"I don't know. Evolution and shit. The big bang."

"Can you explain any of that?"

"Any of what?"

"The big bang."

"It was a bunch of particles and shit that exploded."

"Where'd the particles come from?"

"I don't know. Where'd god come from?"

"He didn't come from nowhere. He's just always been around."

"Well then maybe the particles and stuff have just always been around."

"You don't know what you're talking about."

"No, I don't," I said. "Neither do you. There are zero scientists sitting in this car."

"Hey, you don't need a scientist to figure things out. Just believe what the bible says."

"Ain't there something in there about not stealing?"

"Yeah, there is, which means I'm a bad person. Fine. That don't make the bible wrong about where we all came from."

"But how do you know it's right?"

"How do you know some scientist is right? Be honest, if you don't understand what the hell he's saying, then how can you know he's right?"

"Hey, I trust the people who gave us air conditioning and the internet over the guys who wrote the bible."

"What are you talking about? It's the word of god."

"What does that even mean, word of god? God wrote a book? God writes? Why don't he just come out every morning and tell us what's going on? You know, like a team meeting. 'Okay, you guys over here feed poor people today. And you guys over there need to stop killing each other.' It'd make things easier."

"Now you're just being stupid. He told everybody what to do in the bible. People make their own mistakes. You just read the bible and it'll tell you what to do. You ever read the bible?"

"I tried once. It was worse than when they make you read Beowulf in high school."

I thought that was pretty funny, but Sadie just shook her head.

We rode a little while in silence. Ahead of us was an overpass. As we drove under it, I saw a state trooper's cruiser hiding a little bit off the road. I looked in the rearview mirror. The cruiser pulled away from its spot and got on the road behind us. It wasn't moving fast, though.

"You see that cop?"

She glanced at the speedometer and then at her side mirror. "I'm not speeding. He's not moving to catch up to us."

The cruiser hung back. I kept staring at it in the rearview, but Sadie didn't seem worried about it. "I know what I know," she said.

"What?"

"I know what I know. I don't need someone to tell me what to think."

"Fine. You don't hear me saying you have to think anything. I don't care."

"But you're crapping all over it like I'm stupid. And I'm not. I just know what I know. I feel Jesus in my heart."

"Okay."

"Okay what?"

"Okay, good for you. You feel Jesus in your heart."

"You don't think that means anything?"

"I didn't say that. I don't know what it means. It sounds good in songs and stuff but—"

"Okay, now you're really starting to piss me off. I feel the lord in my heart. I feel him in my heart."

"I don't know what that means," I said. "There's nothing magical about the heart. It's just a wad of tissue. When they bury me, a maggot's gonna eat my heart for dinner and shit it out his ass."

She had both hands together at the top of the steering wheel, and she gripped it like it was about to come off. "You can scoff all you want, but I know what I feel in my heart."

"Hey, cool. Good for you."

Before I could say anything about it she said, "I'd be

dead if it wasn't for Jesus. Did you know that? I had a bottle of Drano in my hands. I was standing in my kitchen, just as sober as you please, and I thought I should just drink it. So I did. I drank it with a bottle of Evan Williams. Passed out. And while I was passed out and dying on my kitchen floor I was granted a vision. I saw all these versions of myself standing in a row, side by side. Me at five years old. Me at ten years old, fifteen, twenty, thirty and so on. And we were all crying. Jesus walked up and kissed each one of us on the forehead. He healed each one of us. I woke up and went to the doctor and got my stomach pumped."

I scratched my head and tried to think of something to say.

"That shut you up," she said.

"Look," I said. "Let's just drop it. If your freaky Drano trip means something to you, then—"

She hit me in the face with her free hand and the car lurched over the right and hit gravel. She pulled it back on the road.

It was all I could do not to slug her. "What the fuck, Sadie?"

She glared at me like she was about to cut my throat. "I don't let any man talk to me that way. My whole life has been one long slog through men's shit. Don't you sit there and blaspheme my vision."

My face stung and I felt all the blood in my body rush to my face. My fists were so tight they hurt. "Listen to me, you cunt. You ever hit me again, I'll fucking kill you."

Sadie didn't say or do anything for about ten seconds. Then she swung at me again. I pulled out of the way and punched her in the side of the head. She jerked the wheel

149

and hit the brakes. A tire popped and rubber thumped against the pavement. We skidded off the road and down into the watery fields of rice, splashing through mud and plants. When we slammed to a stop, the pots in the back hit the floor, and rings and necklaces and cash spilled all over the floorboards.

We sat there blinking as the siren behind us grew louder.

"Oh no," I said. "Oh fuck."

Sadie took a deep breath and leaned back against the seat. She closed her eyes.

"Are you praying?" I yelled.

The cruiser zoomed up on the road behind us. The door flung open.

"No," she said, "but that's a good idea."

OUR VIOLENCE

In June, the heat in Arkansas turns liquid. It seemed to pour in through the windows of my father's little truck as we bumped down a dirt road a few miles outside of town. My brother was squeezed between my father and me, and when Dad pulled over and spread his topographical map across the steering wheel, Russell elbowed me to get out. When I didn't move, he jabbed me harder. Dad threw a glare at us. Then he tapped his map with a thick finger. "This is it," he said. He and I climbed out, but Russell just lay across the bench seat and thumbed through an issue of Captain America.

Dad and I measured off the first lot. He tied some orange tape around a tree and called, "Russ, that's your five acres."

I looked over at Russell. His face was hidden behind the cover of a red, white, and blue superhero bashing in the head of a laser-spewing robot. Russell rolled up the comic and slid out of the truck. Although I was a year older than my brother, he was my exact size. He pointed at the trees. "Over there?"

"Yep," Dad said. "This is the dividing line. Gary's is in the middle here, and five acres that way mine begins." Towering above us, elms and oaks spread out, their branches thick and bent toward the sky like arms waiting to drop. Here and there were a few thin pines.

Russell brushed a gnat from his small, blue eyes, and asked Dad, "What're you gonna do with yours?"

"I'm gonna build a house in another year or so," Dad said. He pulled off his camouflage hunting cap and wiped the sweat from his face with his forearm. "We'll build y'all houses here someday, if you want. Or you can sell it or build something else. Whatever you decide to do with it." Behind him, the sun was low in the trees, and dark spots of red light fell across our faces like specks of blood, and he turned from us and shrugged, slipping his cap back on. He stopped at his truck and paused at the map spread across the hood like a holy text laid across an altar. Russell stood next to him and nodded, looking around as if already envisioning what he would do with his share of the land.

As we were getting ready to leave, and the sun was gone from the sky, but the heat of the day still clung to us like another layer of clothing, Russell and I began to fight over who would sit next to the window. It was a fight we almost always had and one that Russell always lost. I punched him hard in the arm a couple of times to force him to move to the middle of the truck.

Russell would not yield.

"Russell," Dad sighed, "move over and let your brother in."

Russell shook his head. "No," he said. He stared at me when he said it, but I watched Dad.

He scowled and I stepped back. Gritting his teeth, he reached over and slapped Russell's ear. It made a clapping sound, and now the blackened woods behind me seemed loud with frogs and crickets. Russell's eyes turned moist, and his hand jerked up to his ear.

"Move," Dad grunted and Russell slid close to him as I eased in. Russell looked tiny and thin next to Dad, like a shadow with color. Dad glared down at him. "You need to learn to listen and keep your mouth shut." Holding his ear, trying not to cry, Russell nodded quickly.

"Yes sir."

Dad leaned over and thumped me hard on the ear with his middle finger. "You leave your brother alone."

Not rubbing my ear, I nodded. Dad started the truck and Russell drug out his comic book. He leaned in my direction as we rode back home, but as Dad tore down the rut-filled road we all bumped together, the silence between us drowned out by the tires and scattering rocks.

Russell and I didn't talk much about our land in the years that followed. As we broke into our teenage years, we cared less and less about it, but for Dad it was different. While teaching a boys' Sunday School class and working six days a week wiring buildings, he still found the time to clear his land and plan his house. Had my mother been alive to share his joy, it would have been complete. When she died of breast cancer, Russell and I were still very young. It had been just the three of us ever since.

I know that for Dad the land and the house were a culmination of his life's labor. Before we had even cleared the land for the house, he would drive out there after work and walk it in the waning hours of daylight, just thinking, planning and, I think, rejoicing in his blessing. His work, felt in the calluses on his hands, and in the joints of his shoulders and knees, had resulted, finally, in the trees and dirt and grass that spread out before him. He knew that to put a house on it would require even more work. Russell and I knew it too.

We worked a lot for him in those days. Dad was never a baseball-in-the-yard sort of father. Sometimes, when we were younger, he'd wrestle with us in the den, but mostly he took us to work. We grew up holding hammers.

Of the two of us, Russell was the prodigy. He could work like Dad. He moved like him, thought along with him so that Dad never had to ask for a tool without it already being in my brother's hand.

I could do the work okay, I suppose, but even then, in my early teens, I always had my mind on something Brother Charles had said in his sermon the Sunday before. This preoccupation caused my work, more often than not, to suffer. And yet, to my best recollection, my father was lenient with my mistakes. He seemed happy when I'd ask him a theological question he didn't know the answer to, and he would refer many of my inquires to Brother Charles. Dad never seemed to think much of himself as a spiritual authority, but I could tell that, in some way, it made him proud to think that I might someday be one. He regarded my ineptitude at work as an indication, I think, that I was bound for something more important.

When it came to Russell, however, he was far less forgiving.

"Get your head outta your ass," he'd snap. Most of the time Russell would only stare down at his mistake, waiting for Dad to leave so he could cuss his own stupidity. But sometimes he wouldn't contain himself so well, and he'd back talk or sigh as if he were bored. Our father came down hard on these lapses in judgment, and

Russell would end up on the floor or backed against a wall, our father shouting down at him and kicking him in the thighs.

The year I was seventeen, Russell tried out for the football team. I was in choir and, by that time, heavily involved with the youth group at church, but I was excited for Russell. Neither of us had ever been very interested in sports before, but Russell's sudden enthusiasm seemed deeply borne and he threw himself fully into the summer training.

In preparation for the tryouts, he and his friends lifted weights in our backyard. They ran miles in the warm, yellow mornings and slammed into each other in our backyard. Soon, definition showed on Russell's chest and arms. He worked all summer long, exerting a self-control and dedication that I'd never seen him summon before.

Dad didn't seem to notice Russell's new interest very much. After years of wanting to start his own business, he had finally quit his job and done it. He bought all the supplies he knew he would need and got business cards bearing his name underlined with a little lightning bolt. Russell and I had to begin answering the phone, "Phillip Doan Electricity. May I help you?"

About that time my brother became ill and was in bed for a few days. I remember this because his football tryouts were fast approaching and he missed a week of practices. I also remember this because it occurred during Dad's transition between jobs, so he was at home and cared for Russell that week. I passed by Russell's room one afternoon and Dad was placing a cool, wet cloth on my brother's forehead. As my father turned to leave, Russell closed his eyes and smiled. Dad had always been a good caregiver, cleaning sheets, bringing books or movies, and making healthy meals while you slept. His patience with us when we were sick seemed endless, I think, because he experienced our ill health as an echo of our mother's long fight with cancer. I can remember as a small boy his great, rough hand resting on my smooth forehead, hot with fever, and the soothing, reassuring shiver that would sweep over me at his concerned touch. I know Russell felt that shiver as well.

In many ways, these moments of my father's tenderness were the doors that opened our faith to me. I have never had trouble believing that God is a God of love.

In the same way, though, Dad's rage worked toward another end. Though my run-ins with him were far fewer than Russell's, I have known the fear of his descending wrath as well. The sheer physical strength of the man was overwhelming when he was angry. He seemed to tower over you, like Jonathan Edward's angry God, and whether or not you felt you deserved the punishment you paid homage to his sovereignty with your fear. In those moments, everything in the universe disappeared except for your transgressions and his justice. Unlike many people, I've never had trouble reconciling that the God of love is also the God of Hell.

We saw a lot of that side of him during that year. His new business very often kept him working seven days a week, and he seemed to make less money the more he worked. Sometimes he had to take side jobs mending roofs or installing insulation for people at church. He got home some nights at eleven or twelve and would leave before we woke up for school the next morning. Throughout the school year, we had to help him on jobs. We'd walk out of the doors at school, backpacks slung over our shoulders, only to find Dad's truck idling in the circle driveway. Russell would always groan. He didn't complain, of course, but he began to work sloppily and this was the time of his worst clashes with our father.

One humid, late summer day, we were installing the wiring in a big, unfinished house in the middle of town. It was one of the first jobs my dad had been contracted for since beginning his business and we were his only help. Despite the fact that the windows of the house were open, the noonday heat was dreadful. We were standing in what would be the master bedroom and the air was like a pot of warm water. All three of us were covered with sawdust and sweat, and Dad chewed us out for putting the reciprocals too low on the wall. He pushed his cap back and said, "They come in here to Sheetrock in a minute, and they're gonna cut too low cause you got the recep boxes to the damn floor."

Russell's face was wet and red. He put his hands on his hips and jutted his jaw and looked out the window. A tremor went through my hand.

"You listening?" Dad barked. "They're gonna cut 'em too low."

"Well, hot damn," Russell said in a dull voice, "we wouldn't want that."

Dad's lips jerked back and his teeth ground as if he were lifting something heavy. He grabbed Russell and flung him into the wooden skeleton of an interior wall. Then he slapped him twice. The first slap twisted Russell's cap around and shook the skeletal wall. My brother's face was red and pinched. With the second slap, Russell's cap came off and hit me in the thigh. I backed up against an unplugged table saw. Russell covered his face with shaking hands.

157

Dad swatted them away and yelled, "You think this shit's funny, boy?"

Then he stepped back. Sweat fell from his flushed face, and he rubbed his eyes. Then he avoided my sheepish stare as he stomped out of the room.

The front door slammed, and Russell dusted some yellow curls of sawdust from his jeans. He regarded his cap on the floor for a second, but didn't move to pick it up.

I tried to think of something to say, but I was mad at him for some reason. Finally, I walked over to the recep box and pried it loose with the nail claw on my hammer. "'Nother couple inches?" I asked.

Russell picked up his cap and put it on. "Yeah," he said, his blue eyes hot and small. He didn't speak or look at me again as we reapplied the boxes. I knew why.

The physical pain of a whipping is momentary, like a burst of light that swells and fades away, but the embarrassment lasts far longer. The embarrassment, rather than the pain, is the lesson you learn. It is what you come to fear the most. Russell absorbed the beating as if it meant nothing to him because denial was the only weapon left to him.

When Dad came back, we had fixed the boxes. He came in, glancing about the room as if thinking about something else. Russell stood off in the corner, not looking at either of us, and spooled some black cord onto a heavy roll. A few minutes later Dad suggested we break for lunch. We loaded our equipment and went for burgers and cokes.

* * *

Russell did not make the football team that summer. He was strong but he was slow and unfocused in plays. I think that had he tried out any other year, he would have made the cut, but that particular team went to the state playoffs that year, a feat that our school had never pulled off before.

That disappointment changed something in him. He became more distant, less involved in school and church. His friends changed. The meager ambitions of his football crowd were replaced with the non-existent priorities of a new group of boys. They weren't bad kids, really. They weren't especially loud or obnoxious. They were just bored. They were lazy and disconnected and Russell didn't so much join them, as much as he flowed into them, as if his stream had simply carried him into a larger body. I would come home my senior year, and they'd be strewn all over our living room watching television, or playing video games. Occasionally, Russell would coerce one of these guys into suffering through church with him, and together they'd stumble out after services, glassy-eyed and yawning.

At my graduation, Russell and Dad came up to me on the football field. The sun was gone from the evening sky, and all that remained of it were dark red slashes on the horizon. My brother shook my hand like he was a perspective employer and smiled. "Good job, man," he said.

"Yeah, nice hat too," Dad said, nudging him. They laughed at me for being too uptight to throw my hat, and I warmed to their ridicule.

At the end of that summer I moved to Virginia to attend college. Russell graduated the following summer, but he stayed in town. Dad had hoped that Russell would come to work for him after graduation, but instead

Russell went to work loading trucks for Walmart and moved in with a couple of his friends. He bought a truck he couldn't afford and spent the weekends riding around town and getting drunk.

This same period was a time of great transition for my father. He moved into a much more contented phase of his life, just as Russell and I were leaving. By this time his business was doing well, and he had a full-time assistant to help him. He finally built and moved into a new house out on his five acres. He seemed calmer, more cheerful and more thoughtful. Gray appeared at his temples as he passed his forty-fifth birthday, and he was at church more and more often, sitting on committee meetings and going out on visitations. When we spoke, more and more, the conversations turned toward the church.

This culminated when, in the fall of my freshman year at Virginia, he was ordained a deacon. He called me, almost laughing and said, "I'm official now, I guess."

I flew down for the Sunday night ordination service and sat alone on the front pew. Dad sat on the stage behind Brother Charles as the old minister spoke of his charity, responsibility, and upstanding character. Once Dad glanced at the back door and then down at his clasped hands. "We know him," Brother Charles said, "as a man already fulfilling the duties of a deacon. He's a man known to all who know him as one who loves and fears the Lord and who is faithful to his family."

He brought my father to the altar and Dad knelt as Brother Charles called the other eleven deacons together. As the organist softly played, Bother Charles and the deacons laid their hands on Dad and prayed. My father clasped his hands together, praying, and cried.

Russell didn't make it, Dad told me later, because he had to work.

When school let out that winter, I moved in with Dad and did some apprentice pastoring under Brother Charles. One Sunday, Dad and I went up to the church to arrange tables in the Fellowship Hall. We were rolling out a cart of dark brown folding chairs when he asked, "You talk to Russ since you got back?"

"A little," I said. "He told me he'd put in an appearance when I got in town."

"Well, he called and said he's coming over tonight," Dad said. He didn't look at me; his small, blue eyes watched the floor as if he were cautious of tripping over something. "I ain't seen him in a while."

We started unloading the chairs two-by-two. "Not since y'all finished the house?"

"He didn't help me on the house," he said with a snort. "He tell you that?"

"No. I just figured he did."

"He didn't." Dad pulled out a chair. "I never thought I'd raise a lazy son."

I didn't say anything to that. Everything I could think of seemed self-serving.

"He tell you he's got a new girlfriend?" Dad asked.

"No. He didn't mention it. He isn't back with that Walmart cashier is he?"

"Naw," Dad said. "This is a new girl. Lily."

"What's she like?"

"She's pleasant, I reckon. Episcopalian." He shrugged. Dad thought that being an Episcopalian was as close as you could get to being a Catholic without going to Hell.

"He ever bring her to church?"

"He'd have to come to church first."

When Russell came over that night, he looked tired. The weather was turning cold, and when he walked in, he smelled of brittle leaves and cool air. Blond stubble covered his chin, and his eyes were heavy and pink. We sat talking at the kitchen table after Dad had gone to bed, and Russell told me the pitfalls of working for Walmart while we ate cookies and drank coffee.

I asked about Lily.

Russell smiled and scratched the table with a forefinger. "Aww, she's Lily. She works the desk over at Firestone."

"Y'all serious?"

Again, the smile. "I don't know. I guess we are. I love her, you know. She loves me. But I ain't buying a ring anytime soon if that's what you're asking."

I smiled and sipped my coffee. "You mean she's not the one, or you aren't ready?"

Russell's eyes were as serious as a man contemplating a change of religions. "I love her. I'm just not sure that this...that getting married is something I want."

"Well," I said, "if y'all are serious wouldn't it naturally lead to marriage?"

He lowered his head, staring at the table, pulling lightly on the coffee cup without picking it up and said, "Well, we been talking about just moving in together. Maybe getting a place."

"Oh," I said. "Did you tell Dad this?"

He smirked. "Yeah, Gary, he's real excited. No, I haven't told him! I figure I'll wait...a couple of years..."

I shrugged. "Care for a bible study on the sanctity of marriage?"

"Not just now, no," he said. An unsteady smile crept onto his face. "Look. I know he's gonna have a problem with this. I know you do. But we'll be okay. We'll be fine."

I ended up preaching to Russell that night, I guess. But I didn't say anything to Dad the next day, and neither did Russell. A few days later, Russell called me and told me that he was moving in with Lily.

Dad never spoke to me about it, but I knew it wounded him deeply. It wasn't just that Russell was living with a girl he wasn't married to, although that was bad enough. It was that he seemed so calm about it, so distant from the entire system of faith we had been brought up in.

Dad and I were sitting in the den talking one night when Lily and Russell came over. Lily had a round face with affable brown eyes that didn't retain much of what anyone said to her. She and Russell stood in the den with their hands in their pockets and their coats on while Russell tried to act as if nothing were unusual.

My father said, "Why don't y'all sit and stay a while?"

Russell smiled, and they slipped off their coats and draped them over the arm of the sofa. Russell asked how I was, and, as I told him, I watched the way he and Dad glanced at one another, neither listening to what I was saying. This prompted me, for some reason, to babble on at length. When I'd finished, Russell nodded and turned to our father.

"We're thinking about building on my acres next summer," he said.

Dad didn't flinch. It was as if he had been waiting for those exact words. "You are?" he replied.

Russell leaned forward, resting his elbows on his knees. His white face contorted a little as he edged out the words. "Well, we been talking about it."

Dad looked at the carpet for a moment, and then leaned forward in his recliner, sitting almost exactly like Russell, and said, "Here's the deal son. I want to help you but I wouldn't feel right helping you with a house until y'all get married."

Almost before Dad could finish, Russell replied, "That's a pretty poor reason to get married, ain't it? To get a house?"

"I'm not trying to force that. That's up to the two of you, but I love you too much to support you when you're doing something wrong."

It was, I think, the first time I'd ever heard my father say he loved one of us.

Lily smirked and shook her head. I thought she was sneering at Dad, but then Russell sat up straight like she'd prodded him and said, "You gave me the land. It's supposed to be mine."

Dad shrugged and his red, sunburned face was strangely calm, as if he were dealing with someone with a mental illness. "Well, it is yours—and you can do with it what you want—but I can't help you with a house. I can't support you on that. You know that already."

Russell nodded and then, like Dad, he seemed calm. Lily crossed her arms.

"I understand that," Russell said. "I can understand that."

They both grinned nervously and turned away from each other. Then they each looked at me like I was a cloudy mirror. I smiled and changed the subject.

* * *

Russell and Lily bought a doublewide mobile home and drug it out to their land that same winter. I walked over to see it when they had moved in, but Dad wouldn't go. "You go on," he said, heading into his workshop. "I've got things to do out here."

The mobile home was paneled with gray vinyl and sat in a tiny, cramped clearing marked with stumps and stacks of tree limbs. The only step into the home was a cinder block. Inside, the walls were periwinkle and the carpet was a walnut-shade of brown. Over the sofa, a picture of the couple hung next to a portrait of our family. Lily acted as the proud host, showing me room to room, pointing out the garbage disposal and the lights on the vanity mirror, but Russell simply hovered around behind me, his fists buried in his pockets.

A few weeks later, as I was driving home from a Monday Visitation with Brother Charles, I decided to drop by Russell's place. I wound up his narrow path as best as I could and parked next to his navy blue truck. I climbed out of my car and a brutal wind burst through the darkened trees on my land like an attacker and seared into me. I turned my face from its sharp sting, but the winds were so cold they burned my neck and ears.

It had been a dry, snowless winter, and the moon had disappeared behind a curtain of blue-black clouds. A little illumination escaped from the mobile home, but the clearing beyond its meager reach was a black map of roots and ruts. I stumbled to the door, but before I could knock, it jerked open, and Lily scowled down at me. She had on a lime-green shirt with no bra. Her hair was matted and dirty.

"Hi, Lily," I said.

She glared at me for a moment, and then turned and growled into the trailer, "It's your brother."

I climbed up and she jumped out. Coatless, she stomped over to their truck.

Russell staggered from behind the door, unshaven and pale, as she climbed into the truck. "Hold on a minute," he muttered to me, placing his hand on my shoulder. He leaned out the door and the truck's headlights hit him. He yelled, "The fuck you going?"

The truck backed up and tore down the dirt path.

"Shit."

"Trouble in paradise?" I asked.

"Fucking bitch," he muttered. He shut the door and plopped down on the sofa. The room smelled of burnt toast, but I didn't see any. He picked up an old plastic cup from an end table cluttered with magazines and dishes. The cup was decorated with the faded image of a superhero and was full of some mixed drink. After a sip, he bared his teeth and made a biting motion.

He looked up at me. "Sorry," he sighed. "That, you know, that you had to see that with Lily and me."

I sat down beside him "What's wrong with you, Russell?"

"What'd'ya mean?"

"What's wrong with you?"

"Vodka."

He smiled, but I just looked at him. "Gary," he said, "this is just shit between me and her. It don't mean anything. She just went up the road to get some cigarettes. She'll be back in five minutes, though, 'cause there's her wallet on the table. Stupid."

"That's not what I mean, Russ. It's not just this, not

just tonight. You're in pain. You're living in pain."

"Living in pain? Ain't that a little much?" His face was puffy and his eyes were pink. He took a breath in through his nose and lowered his chin to his chest. He stared up at me for a long time. Then he shrugged. "You remember how we used to wrestle with Dad when we were kids?"

"Yeah," I said, annoyed that he was dodging what I said.

"That's...if I had to choose, I'd say those were my favorite childhood memories. Him chunking us all over the place. You remember that? Throwing us on the couch or, you know how he'd flip you off his back real quick, but right before you hit the ground he'd sit you down..." He smiled. "I'll do that with my boys, if I ever have any."

I shook my head. The sound of the truck crept up the road.

"She's back, I guess," I said. "I might need to leave."

He nodded, and I stood up. I wanted to say something profound. I'll pray for you. Think about what I said. Or maybe, I love you. I settled for, "Give me a call."

Outside, Lily was climbing out of the truck. I walked to my car, and she stalked past me but turned around.

"He awake still? Or is he passed out?"

"He's awake."

"Swell," she said.

I drove with the window down over to Dad's house and let the air burn my face. The empty woods between Dad's land and Russell's land, my five acres, were dark, but when I pulled into Dad's drive, his big, high-powered porch light fell across the lawn. The grass sparkled, covered over in a silver mist. When I came in, Dad was watching Red River on television. He turned it off, and we sat at the kitchen table and talked.

I told him what had happened.

His hair was dirty gray, and his wind-burned face was dry and flaked. He rubbed his thick lips with his knuckles and stared at the table. "Russell..." he said. He closed his eyes. "That kid...I don't know how I raised two sons so different. I wasn't a perfect father. I was far from that. But it doesn't make sense that I could raise one right and one wrong. That doesn't seem possible."

I looked down at the table. My reflection was a soft smudge.

Dad rubbed his eyes and sighed. "Maybe if your Mom had lived...that might have changed it all. Maybe I was too easy on him. Or I didn't show him the way to...be. I just wanted him to do what he was supposed to do. I didn't need him to be a preacher." His eyes were pink and, against a face marked by bits of dead skin, they looked painful and hot. "I don't know," he said, but his words were lost in a pounding on the front door.

We frowned at one another and stood up, and I followed him into the den.

Lily stood shaking on the welcome mat, blood seeping from her mouth and soaking her shirt.

Dad put his arm around her and brought her inside. I ran into the kitchen and emptied an ice tray into a yellow hand towel and cleaned off Lily's mouth. Two of her bottom teeth were missing. Her skin was cold and thick, as if the night air had seeped into her. "That son of a bitch," she said. Her pink lips trembled.

"What happened?" I asked.

"I hit him. He hit me back a couple of times. Asshole! He's drunk and pissed."

"About what?" I asked.

My father stood behind her as stiff as a corpse while she rubbed her mouth with a bloody hand. She said, "He's just pissed and I was raggin' him about quitting his job." Her fingers shakily probed her gums, and she began to cry. "He's such a asshole."

Dad turned and walked to the coat rack and pulled on a heavy jacket. He opened the door and walked out onto the porch.

As she watched him walk out, Lily's face went slack. "What's Mr. Doan gonna do?"

I didn't say anything.

A few minutes later, Russell staggered across our father's front lawn and stood a few feet from the porch. His T-shirt was splattered with blood and dirt, and his right hand was bleeding. He shuddered and crystallized breath shot from his nostrils.

"Get out of here," Dad said. He stood rigid, his hands at his sides.

Russell didn't look at him. "Lily!" he yelled. "Get your ass out here."

"Go on," Dad said.

"Lily, get your ass out here!"

Lily ran to the front door. "Go to hell, you son of a bitch!"

Russell's eyes filled with tears. "I can't believe you'd track this up to my daddy's house." He tilted his head back. "Oh God..."

Dad waved his hand at Russell. "Go on, son. Get out of here."

Russell lowered his head and cleared his throat. He looked past Dad and stepped onto the first step. He hadn't looked at our father once. "I'm coming in there, Lily!"

Our father took a step toward him and punched Russell in the face. Russell spun off the step and sprawled on the grass. He pulled himself up, breathing hard and swearing, as if to try for the house again, and Dad stepped down, teeth bared, and struck him twice in the face. The second time, he had to pull Russell up by the shirt to hit him. Russell collapsed as Dad's shadow spilled across him. Then our father stood over him, hands still packed into fists, and Russell began to cry.

I wanted to move, to go help him and hold him. But I didn't. I've always been a coward, but standing there in the doorway watching my father's broad back as my brother cried at his feet, I shamed myself. I did nothing. Whenever I think of sin, I think of that moment.

Lily cried as Russell crawled away on the crunching grass and climbed to his feet. He swayed a moment and then staggered off, his figure bleeding into the trees.

As Dad stood there watching Russell, he seemed oddly thin. Against the trees and the wide lawn, he was tiny, and after a while I could tell that he too was shivering in the frigid night air.

After about ten minutes, we saw the fire. It appeared suddenly out of the forest, the popping of the wood echoing over the rush of incinerating leaves. Orange flames swirled out of the tops of the trees while a quivering, yellow stream of heat poured through the brush and grass. We called the fire department, knowing they could never arrive in time, and we would have to abandon everything and escape by the back road. Lily hid her face and cried in the back seat as we wound through the woods. Tears fell from my father's eyes, but he stared ahead, his body rigid and lifeless. As we fled, we could hear trees snap and fall. I alone turned to see their blackened tops plummet to the earth, their burning red ashes spiraling up into the night sky like the last bursts of confetti at a homecoming celebration.

ACKNOWLEDGMENTS

Previous versions of some of the stories in this collection have been published in the following places:

"Maker's And Coke" and "Night Terrors" appeared in BEAT to A PULP: Round One and BEAT to a PULP: Round Two respectively.

"The Big Sister" appeared online at Mystical-E.

"The Girl from Yesterday" appeared online at Crooked.

"Cold City" appeared as "A Cold Night in Murder City" in issue 3.5 of Crime Factory.

"Aftermath" and "Good Cover" appeared online at Flash Fiction Offensive.

"The Serpent Box" appeared online at Fires On The Plain. I should also note here that this story is a reinterpretation of the Scandinavian fable of "Töre's Daughters In Vänge," most popularly adapted by Ingmar Bergman in the 1960 film The Virgin Spring.

"Dinner with Friends" appeared online at A Twist of Noir.

"Casual Encounter" appeared in Noir Riot.

"The Theologians" appeared in All Due Respect Issue Three.

This collection assembles short fiction written over the course of almost twenty years. In that time, many people helped these stories take shape and find their way into various publications and online venues. As such, I owe many folks a long warm hug. Since—as doubtless many of them already know—I am not a hugger, this written thanks will have to do.

In the Creative Writing program of the University of Arkansas at Little Rock, I would like to thank my first readers: David Jauss, Monica Bergers, Charlie Green, and Jeremy Morphis.

In the Creative Writing program of the University of North Carolina at Wilmington, I need to thank Karen Bender, Wendy Brenner, Clyde Edgerton, Rebecca Lee, and Robert Siegel.

Any thanks extended to the people of UNCW would be incomplete without acknowledging the friendship—and very often the forbearance—of Hannah Dela Cruz Abrams, Patrick Culliton, Chris McSween, and Jay Varner.

A big thanks goes to Christopher Grant at A Twist Of Noir, who published my first crime stories online.

At Beat To A Pulp, I need to thank David Cranmer and Elaine Ash.

At Crime Factory, I need to thank Keith Rawson, Andrew Nette, Cameron Ashley, and Liam Jose.

At Fires On The Plain and Noir Riot, a great thanks to Cullen Gallagher.

At Noir Riot and NoirCon, a big thank you to the great Lou Boxer.

Finally, a huge thanks to Chris Rhatigan and Mike Monson at All Due Respect. You guys are the best.

Award-winning novelist Jake Hinkson was born and raised in Arkansas. He has written articles and profiles for *The Los Angeles Review of Books*, *Mental Floss*, and *Noir City*, and he is the author of the essay collection *The Blind Alley: Exploring Film Noir's Forgotten Corners*. His books have been translated into French and Italian, and he has received the two most prestigious awards granted to literary crime fiction in France: in 2016, his novel *Hell on Church Street* (*L'Enfer de Church Street*) was awarded the Prix Mystère de la Critique, and his novel *No Tomorrow* (*Sans Lendemain*) was awarded the Grand Prix des Littératures Policières in 2018. He lives in Chicago.

BOOKS

On the following pages are a few
more great titles from the
Down & Out Books publishing family.

For a complete list of books and to
sign up for our newsletter,
go to DownAndOutBooks.com.

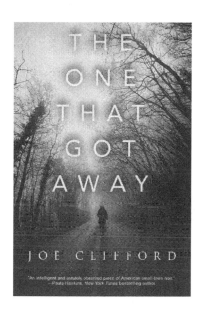

The One That Got Away
Joe Clifford

Down & Out Books
978-1-948235-42-6

In the early 2000s, a string of abductions rocked the small upstate town of Reine, New York. Only one girl survived: Alex Salerno. The killer was sent away. Life returned to normal. No more girls would have to die.

Until another one did...

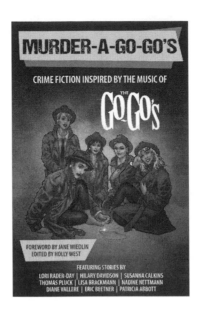

Murder-A-Go-Go's
Crime Fiction Inspired by the Music of The Go-Go's
Edited by Holly West

Down & Out Books
978-1-948235-62-4

The Go-Go's made music on their own terms and gave voice to a generation caught between the bra-burning irreverence of the seventies and the me-first decadence of the eighties.

With a foreword by Go-Go's co-founder Jane Wiedlin and original stories by twenty-five kick-ass authors, editor Holly West has put together an all-star crime fiction anthology.

Gravy Train
Tess Makovesky

All Due Respect, an imprint of
Down & Out Books
978-1-64396-006-7

When barmaid Sandra wins eighty grand on a betting scam she thinks she's got it made. But she's reckoned without an assortment of losers and criminals, including a mugger, a car thief and even her own step-uncle George.

As they hurtle towards a frantic showdown by the local canal, will Sandra see her ill-gotten gains again? Or will her precious gravy train come shuddering to a halt?

The Lucky Clover
Nick Heeb

Shotgun Honey, an imprint of
Down & Out Books
978-1-948235-69-3

When the Narrator returns to his old haunt, The Lucky Clover, he is looking to forget and recover from his past life's miseries and humiliations by drinking with good friends.

He soon discovers the people closest to him had no interest in his honest intentions, and that violence is the only language spoken in this sparse and hard country he calls home.